Not the First Murder—
Nor the Last

Hawk sat bolt upright in his chair as a scream rang out on the landing—and was suddenly cut short. He grabbed his axe and ran, followed closely by Fisher. The first scream had been a man's, but now a woman was screaming, on and on . . .

The victim lay twisted on the floor, his eyes wide and staring. His clothes were splashed with blood, and more had soaked into the carpet around him. His throat had been torn out.

HAWK & FISHER
The war against crime is forever.

HAWK & FISHER

SIMON GREEN

ACE BOOKS, NEW YORK

This book is an Ace original edition,
and has never been previously published.

HAWK & FISHER

An Ace Book / published by arrangement with
the author

PRINTING HISTORY
Ace edition / September 1990

ISBN: 0-441-58417-9

Ace Books are published by The Berkley Publishing Group,
200 Madison Avenue, New York, NY 10016.
The name ''ACE'' and the ''A'' logo
are trademarks belonging to Charter Communications, Inc.

PRINTED IN THE UNITED STATES OF AMERICA

10 9 8 7 6 5 4 3 2 1

HAWK & FISHER

Some things can never be forgiven.

1

A Hidden Darkness

Haven is a dark city.

The narrow streets huddled together, the plain stone and timber buildings leaning on each other for support. Out-leaning upper storeys bowed to each other like tired old men, shutting out the light, but even in the shadows there was little relief from the midsummer heat. The glaring sun scorched down on the sprawling city, driving all moisture from the air. The streets were parched and dusty and thick with buzzing flies. Being a seaport, Haven usually got all the rain it wanted, and then some, but not in midsummer. The long days wore on, and the baking heat made them a misery of sweat and thirst and endless fatigue. The days were too hot to work and the nights too hot to sleep. Tempers grew short and frayed, but it was too hot to brawl. Birds hung on the sky like drifting shadows, but there was never a trace of a cloud or a breeze. Haven at midsummer was a breeding ground for trouble. The heat stirred men's minds and brought forth hidden evils. Everyone watched the skies and prayed for rain, and still the long dry summer dragged on.

Hawk and Fisher, Captains in the city Guard, strolled unhurriedly down Chandler Lane, deep in the rotten heart of the North side. It was too hot to hurry. The grimy, overshadowed lane was a little cooler than most, which meant the heat was only mildly unbearable. Flies hovered over piles of garbage and swarmed around the open sewers. The squat and ugly buildings were black with soot from the nearby tannery, and the muggy air smelt strongly of smoke and tannin.

Hawk was tall, dark, and no longer handsome. He wore a black silk patch over his right eye, and a series of old scars ran down the right side of his face, showing pale against the tanned skin. He wore a simple cotton shirt and trousers, but didn't bother with the black Guardsman's cloak required by regulations. It was too hot for a cloak, and anyway, he didn't need one to tell people he was a Guard. Everyone in Haven had heard of Captain Hawk.

He didn't look like much. He was lean and wiry rather than muscular, and he was beginning to build a stomach. He wore his dark hair at shoulder length, swept back from his forehead and tied with a silver clasp. He had only just turned thirty, but already there were a few streaks of grey in his hair. At first glance he looked like just another bravo, not as young as he once was, perhaps a little past his prime. But few people stopped at the first glance; there was something about Hawk, something in his scarred face and single cold eye that gave even the drunkest hardcase pause. On his right hip Hawk carried a short-handled axe instead of a sword. He was very good with an axe.

Captain Fisher walked at Hawk's side, echoing his pace and stance with the naturalness of long companionship. Isobel Fisher was tall, easily six feet in height, and her long blond hair fell to her waist in a single thick plait. She was in her mid to late twenties, and handsome rather than beautiful. There was a rawboned harshness to her face that contrasted strongly with her deep blue eyes and generous mouth. Like Hawk, she wore a cotton shirt and trousers, and no cloak. The shirt was half-unbuttoned to show a generous amount of bosom, and her shirt sleeves were rolled up, revealing arms corded with muscle and lined with old scars. She wore a sword on her hip, and her hand rested comfortably on the pommel.

Hawk and Fisher; partners, husband and wife, guardians of the city law. Known, respected, and mostly feared throughout Haven, even in the lower Northside, where the very rats went round in pairs for safety. Hawk and Fisher were the best, and everyone knew it. They were honest and hard-working, a rare combination in Haven, but more important still, they were dangerous.

Hawk looked about him and scowled slightly. Chandler Lane was deserted, with not a soul in sight, and that was . . . unusual. The afternoon was fast turning into evening, but even so there should have been people out selling and buying and making a deal. On the lower Northside everything was for sale, if you knew where to look. But all around, the doors and shutters were firmly closed despite the stifling heat, and the shadows lay still and undisturbed. It was like looking at a street under siege. Hawk smiled sourly. If his information was correct, that might just be the case.

"There's going to be a full moon tonight," said Fisher quietly.

Hawk nodded. "That'll bring out the crazies. Though how anyone has the energy even to plan a crime in this heat is beyond me."

"You do realise this is probably nothing more than a wild goose chase, don't you?"

"Not again, Isobel, please. The word is he's hiding right here, at the end of this street. We have to check it out."

"Three months," said Fisher angrily. "Three months we've been working on that child prostitution racket. And just when we're starting to get somewhere, what happens? The word comes down from Above, and we get pulled off the case to go looking for a vampire!"

"Yeah," said Hawk. "And all because we raided the Nag's Head. Still, I'd do it again, if I had to."

Fisher nodded grimly.

The Nag's Head was a hole-in-the-wall tavern on Salt Lane, just on the boundary of the Eastside slums. The upper floor was a brothel, and the word was that they were interested in acquiring children. Cash in hand, no questions asked. Child prostitution had been illegal in Haven for almost seven years, but there were still those with a vested interest in keeping the market open. Like many other places, the Nag's Head kept itself in business by greasing the right palms, but one man had made the mistake of trying to buy off Hawk and Fisher. So they had paid the place a visit.

The bravo at the door tried to bar their way. He was either new in town, or not particularly bright. Hawk gave him a straight-finger jab under the sternum. The bravo's face went very pale and he bent slowly forward, almost as though bowing to Hawk. Fisher waited till he was bent right over, and then rabbit-punched him. The bravo went down without a murmur. Hawk and Fisher stepped cautiously over him, kicked in the door, and burst into the Nag's Head with cold steel in their hands.

The staff and patrons took one look at them and a sudden silence fell over the crowded room. Smoke curled on the stuffy air, and the watching eyes were bright with fear and suppressed anger. Hawk and Fisher headed for the stairs at the back of the dimly lit room, and a pathway opened up before them as people got hurriedly out of their way. Three bravos crowded together at the foot of the stairs with drawn swords. They were big, muscular men with cold, calculating eyes who knew how to use their swords. Hawk cut down two of them with his axe while Fisher stabbed the third cleanly through the heart. They stepped quickly over the bodies and pounded up the stairs. The upper floor was ominously quiet. Hawk and Fisher charged along the narrow landing, kicking open doors as they went, but most of the occupants were long gone, having disappeared down the fire escape at the first sound of trouble.

One of the prostitutes hadn't been able to get away. Hawk found her in the last room but one. She was dressed in torn silks too large for her, and wore gaudy colors on her face. She was chained to the wall by the throat, and her back ran red from the wounds of a recent whipping. She sat slumped against the wall, her face pressed against the rough wood, crying softly, hopelessly. She was almost twelve years old.

Fisher joined Hawk in the doorway, and swore angrily as she took in the scene. The chain was too heavy to break, so Hawk levered the bolt out of the wall with his axe. Fisher tried to comfort the child, but she was too frightened to say much. She'd been abducted in the street two years ago, and been brought to this room. Her abductors put the chain around her neck and locked it, and she'd never been out of the room since. Both Hawk and Fisher told her she was free now, but she didn't believe it. *There's a man who comes to visit me*, she said quietly. *He was here today. He'll never let me go. You can't protect me from him. No one can. He's important.*

She didn't know his name. No one ever told her their name.

Hawk and Fisher never did find out who he was, but he must have had influence. Only two days later, the child was stabbed to death in the street. Her attacker was never found. Hawk and Fisher were officially taken off the case and sent to join the other Guards searching for the supposed vampire that was terrorising the Northside. They raised hell with their superiors, and even talked about quitting the Guard, but none of it did any good. The word had come down from somewhere high Above, and there was no arguing with it. Hawk and Fisher had shrugged and cursed and finally given up. There would be other times.

Besides, it seemed there really was a vampire. Men, women, and children had been attacked at night, and occasionally bodies were found with no blood left in them. There were dozens of sightings and as many suspects, but none of them led anywhere. And then a lamplighter had come to see Hawk, and there was no denying the horror in his voice as he told Hawk and Fisher of the dark figure he'd seen crawling up the outside of the house in Chandler Lane. . . .

"All the Guards in Haven, and that man had to choose us to tell his story to," grumbled Fisher. "Why us?"

"Because we're the best," said Hawk. "So obviously we're not afraid to tackle anything. Even a vampire."

Fisher sniffed. "We should have settled for second best."

"Not in my nature," said Hawk easily. "Or yours."

They chuckled quietly together. The low, cheerful sound seemed out of place in the silence. For the first time Hawk realised just how quiet the empty street was. It was like walking through the empty shell of some village abandoned by its people but not yet overgrown by the Forest. The only sound was his and Fisher's footsteps, echoing dully back from the thick stone walls to either side of them. Despite the heat, Hawk felt a sudden chill run down his back, and the sweat on his brow was suddenly cold. Hawk shook his head angrily. This was no time to be letting his nerves get the better of him.

Hawk and Fisher finally came to a halt before a decrepit two-storey building almost at the end of the lane. Paint was peeling from the closed front door, and the stonework was pitted and crumbling. The two narrow windows were hidden behind closed wooden shutters. Hawk looked the place over and frowned thoughtfully. There was something disquieting about the house, something he couldn't quite put a name to. It was like a sound so quiet you almost missed it, or a scent so faint you could barely smell it. . . . Hawk scowled, and let his hand fall to the axe at his side.

Vampire . . . revenant . . . that which returns . . .

He'd never seen one of the undead, and didn't know anyone who had. He wasn't altogether sure he believed in such things, but then, he didn't disbelieve in them either. In his time he'd known demons and devils, werewolves and undines, and faced them all with cold steel in his hand. The world had its dark places, and they were older by far than anything man had ever built. And there was no denying that people had disappeared from the Northside of late . . . and one person in particular.

"Well?" said Fisher.

Hawk looked at her irritably. "Well what?"

"Well, are we going to just stand here all afternoon, or are we going to do something? In case you hadn't noticed, the sun's getting bloody low on the sky. It'll be dark inside an hour. And if there really is a vampire in there . . ."

"Right. The undead rise from their coffins when the sun is down." Hawk shivered again, and then smiled slightly as he took in the goose flesh on Fisher's bare arms. Neither of them cared much for the dark, or the creatures that moved in it. Hawk took a deep breath, stepped up to the front door, and knocked loudly with his fist.

"Open in the name of the Guard!"

There was no response. Silence lay across the empty street like a smothering blanket, weighed down by the heat. Hawk wiped at the sweat running down his face with the back of his hand, and wished he'd brought a water canteen. He also wished he'd followed regulations for once and waited for a backup team, but there hadn't been time. They had to get to the vampire while he still slept. And besides, Councillor Trask's daughter was still missing. Which was why finding the vampire had suddenly become such a high priority. As long as he'd kept to the poorer sections of the city, and preyed only on those who wouldn't be missed, no one paid much attention to him. But once he snatched a Councillor's daughter out of her own bedroom, in full view of her screaming mother . . . Hawk worried his lower lip between his teeth. She should still be alive. Vampires were supposed to take two to three days to drain a victim completely, and she couldn't become one of the undead until she'd died and risen again. At least, that was what the legends said. Hawk sniffed. He didn't put much trust in legends.

"We should have stopped off and picked up some garlic," he said suddenly. "That's supposed to be a protection, isn't it?"

"Garlic?" said Fisher. "At this time of the year? You know how much that stuff costs in the markets? It has to come clear across the country, and the merchants charge accordingly."

"All right, it was just a thought. I suppose hawthorn is out as well."

"Definitely."

"I assume you have at least brought the stake with you? In fact, you'd better have the stake, because I'm bloody well not going in there without one."

"Relax, love. I've got it right here." Fisher pulled a thick wooden stake from the top of her boot. It was over a foot long, and had been roughly sharpened to a point. It looked brutally efficient. "As I understand it, it's quite simple," said Fisher briskly. "I hammer this through the vampire's heart, and then you cut off his head. We burn the two parts of the body separately, scatter the ashes, and that's that."

"Oh, sure," said Hawk. "Just like that." He paused a moment, looking at the closed door before him. "Did you ever meet Trask, or his daughter?"

"I saw Trask at the briefing yesterday," said Fisher, slipping the stake back into her boot. "He looked pretty broken up. You know them?"

"I met his daughter a few months back. Just briefly. I was bodyguarding Councillor DeGeorge at the time. Trask's daughter had just turned sixteen, and she looked so . . . bright, and happy."

Fisher put her hand on his arm. "We'll get her back, Hawk. We'll get her back."

"Yeah," said Hawk. "Sure."

He hammered on the door again with his fist. *Do it by the book. . . .* The sound echoed on the quiet, and then died quickly away. There was no response from the house, or from any of its neighbours. Hawk glanced up and down the empty street. It could always be a trap of some kind. . . . No. His instincts would have been screaming at him by now. After four years in the city Guard, he had good instincts. Without them, you didn't last four years.

"All right," he said finally. "We go in. But watch your

back on this one, lass. We take it one room at a time, by the book, and keep our eyes open. Right?"

"Right," said Fisher. "But we should be safe enough as long as the sun's up. The vampire can't leave his coffin till it's dark."

"Yeah, but he might not be alone in there. Apparently most vampires have a human servant to watch over them while they sleep. A kind of Judas Goat, a protector who also helps to lure victims to his master."

"You've been reading up on this, haven't you?" said Fisher.

"Damn right," said Hawk. "Ever since the first rumours. I wasn't going to be caught unprepared, like I was on that werewolf case last year."

He tried the door handle. It turned jerkily in his hand, and the door swung slowly open as he applied a little pressure. The hinges squealed protestingly, and Hawk jumped despite himself. He pushed the door wide open and stared into the dark and empty hall. Nothing moved in the gloom, and the shadows stared silently back. Fisher moved softly in beside Hawk, her hand resting on the pommel of her sword.

"Strange the door wasn't locked," said Hawk. "Unless we were expected."

"Let's get on with it," said Fisher quietly. "I'm starting to get a very bad feeling about this."

They stepped forward into the hall and then closed the front door behind them, leaving it just a little ajar. Never know when you might need a quick exit. Hawk and Fisher stood together in the gloom, waiting for their eyes to adjust. Hawk had a stub of candle in his pocket, but he didn't want to use it unless he had to. All it took was a sudden gust of wind at the wrong moment and the light would be gone, leaving him blind and helpless in the dark. Better to

let his sight adjust while he had the chance. He heard
Fisher stir uneasily beside him, and he smiled slightly. He
knew how she felt. Patiently standing and waiting just
wasn't in their nature; they always felt better when they
were doing something. Anything. Hawk glared about him
into the gloom. There could be someone hiding in the
shadows, watching them, and they'd never know it until it
was too late. Something could already be moving silently
towards them, with reaching hands and bared fangs. . . .
He felt his shoulders growing stiff and tense, and made
himself breathe deeply and slowly. It didn't matter what
was out there; he had his axe and he had Fisher at his
side. Nothing else mattered. His eyesight slowly grew used
to the gloom, and the narrow hall gradually formed itself
out of the shadows. It was completely empty. Hawk relaxed a little.

"You all right?" he whispered to Fisher.

"Yeah, fine," she said quietly. "Let's go."

The hall ended in a bare wooden stairway that led up
to the next floor. Two doors led off from the hall, one to
each side. Hawk drew his axe, and hefted it in one hand.
The heavy weight of it was reassuring. He glanced at
Fisher, and smiled as he saw the sword in her hand. He
caught her eye, and gestured for her to take the right-hand
door while he took the left. She nodded, and padded quietly over to the right.

Hawk listened carefully at his door, but everything was
quiet. He turned the handle, eased the door open an inch,
and then kicked it in. He leapt into the room and glared
quickly about him, his axe poised and ready. The room
was empty. There was no furniture, and all the walls were
bare. A little light filtered past the closed shutters, taking
the edge off the gloom. The woodwork was flecked with
mould, and everywhere was thick with dust. There was

no sign to show the room had ever been lived in. The floorboards creaked loudly under Hawk's weight as he walked slowly forward. There was a strong smell of dust and rotten wood, but underneath that there was a faint but definite smell of corruption, as though something long dead lay buried close at hand. Hawk sniffed at the air, but couldn't decide if the smell was really there or if he was just imagining it. He moved quickly round the room, tapping the walls and listening to the echo, but there was no trace of any hidden panel or passageway. Hawk stood in the middle of the room, looking around him to check he hadn't missed anything, and then went back into the hall.

Fisher was waiting for him. He shook his head, and Fisher shrugged disappointedly. Hawk smiled slightly. He already knew Fisher hadn't found anything; if she had, he'd have heard the sound of battle. Fisher wasn't known for her diplomacy. Hawk started towards the stairs, and Fisher moved quickly in beside him.

The bare wooden steps creaked and groaned beneath their feet, and Hawk scowled. If there was someone here, watching over the vampire, they had to know there was someone else in the house. You couldn't put your foot down anywhere without some creaking board giving away your position. He hurried up the rest of the stairs and out onto the landing. He felt a little less vulnerable on the landing; there was more room to move, if it came to a fight. The floor was thick with dust and rat droppings, and the bare wooden walls were dull and scarred. Two doors led off from the landing, to their right. It was just as gloomy as the ground-floor hall, and Hawk thought fleetingly of his candle before deciding against it. If the sound hadn't given them away, a light certainly would. He moved over to stand before the first door, and listened carefully. He couldn't hear anything. Hawk smiled slightly. If this house did turn out to be empty, he was going to feel bloody ridiculous. He looked at Fisher, and gestured for her to guard his back. She nodded quickly. Hawk tried the door handle, and it turned easily in his grasp. He pushed the door slightly ajar, took a deep breath, and kicked the door in.

He darted forward into the room, axe at the ready, and again there was no one there. Without looking around, Hawk knew that Fisher was looking at him knowingly.

I said this was a wild goose chase, Hawk. . . .

He didn't look back. He wouldn't give her the satisfaction. He glared about him, taking in the darkened room. A sparse light seeped past the closed shutters to show him a wardrobe to his left and a bed to his right. A large wooden chest stood at the foot of the bare bed. Hawk eyed the chest suspiciously. It looked to be a good four feet long and three feet wide; quite large enough to hold a body. Hawk frowned. Like it or not, he was going to need some light to check the room out properly. He peered about him, and his gaze fell on an old oil lamp lying on the floor by the bed. He bent down, picked the lamp up and shook it gently. He could feel oil sloshing back and forth in the base of the lamp. Hawk worried his lower lip between his teeth. The house might appear deserted, but somebody had to have been here recently. . . . He took out flint and steel and lit the lamp. The sudden golden glow made the room seem smaller and less threatening.

Hawk moved over to the chest and crouched down before it. There didn't seem to be any lock or bolts. He glanced at Fisher, who took a firm hold on the wooden stake in her left hand and nodded for him to try the lid. He clutched his axe tightly, and then threw the lid open. Hawk let out his breath in a slow sigh of relief, and he and Fisher relaxed a little as they took in the pile of old bed linen that filled the chest. The cloth was flecked with a rather nasty-looking mould, and had obviously been left in the chest for ages, but Hawk rummaged gingerly through it anyway, just in case there might be something hidden under it. There wasn't. Hawk wiped his hands thoroughly on his trousers.

All this taking it slow and easy was getting on his nerves. He suddenly wanted very badly just to run amok and tear the place apart until he found the missing girl, but he knew he couldn't do that. Firstly, if there was no one here the house's owners would sue his arse in the courts, and secondly, if there was a vampire here he was bound to be well hidden, and nothing less than a careful, methodical search was going to find him.

One room at a time, one thing at a time, by the book. Follow the procedures. And he and Fisher might just get out of this alive yet.

He moved over to the bed and got down on his hands and knees to look underneath it. A big hairy spider darted out of the shadows towards him, and he fell backwards with a startled yelp. The spider quickly disappeared back into the shadows. Hawk quickly regained his balance and shot a dirty look at Fisher, who was trying hard not to laugh and only just making it. Hawk growled something under his breath, picked up the lamp from the floor and swept it back and forth before him. There was nothing under the bed but dust.

Not in the chest, and not under the bed. That only left the wardrobe, though it seemed a bit obvious. Hawk clambered to his feet, put the lamp on the chest, and moved over to stand before the wardrobe. It was a big piece of furniture, almost seven feet tall and four feet wide. *Wonder how they got it up the stairs?* thought Hawk absently. He took a firm hold on the door handle, gestured for Fisher

to stand ready, and then jerked open the door. Inside the
wardrobe a teenage girl was hanging naked from a butcher's hook. Her eyes were wide and staring, and she'd been
dead for some time. Two jagged puncture wounds showed
clearly on her throat, bright red against the white skin.
The steel tip of the butcher's hook protruded from her
right shoulder, just above the collarbone. No blood had
run from the wound, suggesting she was already dead when
the hook went into her. Hawk swallowed hard and reached
forward to gently touch the dead girl's hand. The flesh was
icy cold.

"Damn," he said quietly. "Oh, damn."

"It's her, isn't it?" said Fisher. "Councillor Trask's
daughter."

"Yes," said Hawk. "It's her."

"The vampire must have been thirsty. Or maybe just
greedy. I doubt there's a drop of blood left in her body."

"Look at her," said Hawk harshly. "Sixteen years old,
and left to hang in darkness like a side of beef. She was
so pretty, so alive. . . . She didn't deserve to die like this.
No one deserves to die like this."

"Easy," said Fisher softly. "Take it easy, love. We'll
get the bastard that did this. Now let's get the girl down."

"What?" Hawk looked at Fisher confusedly.

"We have to get her down, Hawk," said Fisher. "She
died from a vampire's bite. If we leave her, she'll rise
again as one of the undead. We can spare her that, at
least."

Hawk nodded slowly. "Yes. Of course."

Somehow, between them, they got the body off the hook
and out of the wardrobe. They laid the dead girl out on
the bed, and Hawk tried to close the staring eyes. They
wouldn't stay shut, and in the end Fisher put two coins on
the eyes to hold the lids down.

"I don't even know her name," said Hawk. "I only knew her as Trask's daughter."

The scream caught him off guard, and he'd only just started to turn round when a heavy weight slammed into him from behind. He and his attacker fell sprawling on the floor, and the axe flew out of Hawk's hand. He slammed his elbow back into his attacker's ribs and pulled himself free. He scrambled away and went after his axe. The attacker lurched to his feet, and Fisher stepped forward to run him through with her sword. The man dodged aside at the last moment and grabbed Fisher's extended arm. She groaned aloud as his fingers crushed her arm, grinding the muscles against the bone. Her sword fell from her numbed fingers. She clawed at his hand, and couldn't move it. He was strong, impossibly strong, and she couldn't tear herself free. . . .

He flung her away from him. She slammed against the far wall and slid dazedly to the floor. Hawk started forward, axe in hand, and then stopped dead as he finally saw who his attacker was.

"Trask . . ." Hawk gaped at the nondescript, middle-aged man standing grinning before him. The Councillor was little more than medium height and painfully thin, but his eyes burned in his gaunt face.

"She was your daughter, you bastard!" said Hawk. "Your own daughter . . ."

"She will live forever," said Trask, his voice horribly calm and reasonable. "So will I. My master has promised me this. My daughter was afraid at first; she didn't understand. But she will. We will never grow old and ugly and die and lie forever in the cold earth. We will be strong and powerful and everyone will fear us. All I have to do is protect the master from fools like you."

He darted forward, and Hawk met him with his axe. He

swung it double-handed with all his strength, and the wide metal blade punched clean through Trask's ribs. The Councillor screamed, as much with rage as with pain, and staggered back against the bed. Hawk pulled his axe free and got ready to hit him again if necessary. Trask looked down at his ribs, and saw the blood that flowed from the gaping wound in his side. He dipped his fingers into the blood, lifted them to his mouth and licked them clean. Hawk lifted his axe and Trask went for his throat. Hawk fought for breath as Trask's bony fingers closed around his throat and tightened. He tried to swing his axe, but he couldn't use it at such close quarters. He dropped it, and grabbed Trask's wrists, but the Councillor was too strong. Hawk's gaze began to dim. He could hear his blood pounding in his ears.

Fisher stepped in beside them and cut at Trask's right arm with her sword. The gleaming blade sliced through the muscle, and the arm went limp. Hawk gathered the last of his strength and pushed Trask away from him. Trask lashed out at Fisher with his undamaged arm. She ducked under the blow and ran her sword through his heart with a single thrust. Trask stood very still, looking down at the gleaming steel blade protruding from his chest. Fisher jerked it out, and Trask collapsed, as though only the sword had been holding him up. He lay on his back on the floor, blood pooling around his body, and glared silently up at Hawk and Fisher. And then the light went out of his eyes, and his breathing stopped.

Hawk leaned back against the wall and felt gingerly at his bruised throat. Fisher stirred Trask's body with her boot, and when he didn't react, knelt down beside him and felt cautiously for a pulse. There wasn't one. Fisher nodded, satisfied, and got to her feet again.

"He's gone, Hawk. The bastard's dead."

"Good," said Hawk, and frowned at how rough his voice sounded. He wouldn't have minded, but it felt even worse than it sounded. "You all right, lass?"

"I've felt worse. Could Trask be the vampire, do you think?"

"No," said Hawk. "He hasn't got the teeth for it. Besides, we saw him at the briefing yesterday morning, remember?"

"Yeah, right. Trask was just the Judas Goat. But I think we'd better stake him anyway. Just to be sure."

"Let's see to the girl first."

"Sure."

Hawk pounded the stake into her heart. It was hard work. He let Fisher stake Trask, while he cut off the girl's head as cleanly as he could. There was no blood, but that somehow made it worse. Cutting off Trask's head was no problem at all. When it was finished, Hawk and Fisher left the room and shut the door quietly behind them. Hawk had thought the air would smell fresher on the landing, but it didn't. He held up the oil lamp he'd brought from the room, and studied the next door in its flickering light.

"He has to be in there somewhere," said Fisher quietly.

Hawk nodded slowly. He looked at her, and then frowned as he saw she was holding a wooden stake in her left hand. "How many of those did you bring?"

"Three," said Fisher calmly. "I used two on Trask and his daughter. If there's more than one vampire here, we're in big trouble."

Hawk smiled in spite of himself. "You always did have a gift for understatement."

He opened the door a crack, stepped back a pace and then kicked the door in. It flew back to slam against the inner wall, and the sound was very loud on the quiet. The echoes took a long time to die away. Hawk stepped cautiously into the room, his axe in one hand and the lamp in the other. The room was empty, save for a heavy metal bed pushed up against the far wall. Fisher moved slowly round the room, tapping the walls and looking for hidden panels. Hawk stood in the middle of the room, and glared about him. *He's here somewhere. He has to be here somewhere.* He moved over to the bed, and looked underneath it. Nothing but dust and shadows. He straightened up and looked at Fisher. She shook her head and looked uneasily about her. Hawk scowled, and looked back at the bed. And then he smiled slowly as an idea came to him.

"Isobel, give me a hand with this."

Between them they got the bed away from the wall, and Hawk studied the wall panelling carefully in the light from his lamp. He smiled grimly as he made out the lines of a hidden panel, fitted his axe blade into one of the cracks, and applied a slow pressure. The wood creaked and groaned loudly, and then a whole section of the wall swung open on a concealed hinge. Behind the panel was a hidden compartment, and in that compartment lay a huge coffin. Hawk felt his mouth go dry, just looking at it. The coffin was seven feet long and three feet wide, built from a dark red wood Hawk didn't recognise. Glyphs and runes had been carved into the sides and lid. He didn't recognise them either. Hawk looked at Fisher, standing close beside him. Her face was very pale.

"Come on," he said quietly. "Let's get it out of there."

The coffin was even heavier than it looked. They had to drag it into the room, inch by inch. It smelled bad. It smelled of blood and death and decay, and Hawk had to keep turning his head away in search of fresher air. He and Fisher finally got the coffin out of the hidden compartment and into the room, then stepped back to take a look at it.

"Big, isn't it?" said Fisher softly.

"Yeah," said Hawk. "Look, as soon as I get the lid open, you get that stake into him. As soon as the stake's home, I'll cut off the head. I'm not taking any chances with this one."

"Got it," said Fisher. "We've been on some dirty jobs in the past, Hawk, but this has got to be the dirtiest."

"Remember the girl," said Hawk. "Now, let's do it."

They bent over the coffin and the lid flew open, knocking them both backwards. The vampire sat up in its coffin and grinned at them with pointed teeth. Hawk's hand tightened round the haft of his axe till his fingers ached. He'd thought he knew what a vampire would look like, but he'd been wrong. The creature before him might once have been a man, but it wasn't anymore. It looked like what it was; something that had died and been buried, and then dug its way up out of the grave. Its face was sunken and wrinkled, and there was a bluish tinge to the dead white skin. The eyes were a dirty yellow, without pupil or retina, as though the eyeballs had rotted in their sockets. A few wisps of long white hair frayed away from the bony skull. The hands were horribly thin, the fingers little more than claws. But the real horror lay in subtler things. The vampire's black robes were rotting and falling apart. Graveyard lichens and moss grew here and there on the dead skin. Its chest didn't move, because it no longer needed to breathe. And it smelled like rotting meat that had been left to hang too long.

It rose up from its coffin in a single smooth movement and looked at Hawk and Fisher with its empty yellow eyes. Hawk looked away despite himself, and his gaze fell on the shuttered window. No light showed around the shutters' edges. *We left it too late! The sun's gone down. . . .*

The vampire stepped elegantly out of its coffin. Its bare feet made no sound on the wooden floor.

Fisher wrinkled her nose at the smell. "Dirty stinking bastard. Lying down or standing up, it makes no difference. Let's do it, Hawk."

Hawk nodded slowly, and then sprang forward, swinging his axe double-handed at the vampire's neck. The creature put up a spindly arm to block the blow, and the axe bounced off, vibrating as though it had struck an iron bar. Hawk's hands went numb from the impact, and it was all he could do to hang onto the axe. Fisher thrust at the vampire with her stake, using it like a dagger. The vampire avoided the blow easily, and knocked Fisher sprawling with a single backhanded blow. She lay where she had fallen, her head swimming madly. There was an inhuman power in the creature's slender frame. Fisher clutched desperately at the wooden stake, and struggled weakly to get her feet under her. The vampire looked down at her and chuckled suddenly—a low, filthy sound.

Hawk swung his axe at it again. The vampire raised its head and caught the heavy blade in mid-swing, wrenching the weapon from Hawk's hand. It threw the axe away, and reached for Hawk with its bony hands. He darted back out of range and looked desperately about him for another weapon. The vampire laughed again, and bent over Fisher. It grabbed her by the shoulder, and she moaned aloud as the clawlike fingers sank into her flesh. Blood ran down her arm in a steady stream. She tried to break free, and couldn't. The vampire drew her slowly closer, grinning widely to show her its long pointed teeth. Fisher tried again to stab the vampire with the stake. It grabbed her wrist and squeezed hard. The feeling went out of her fingers and she dropped the stake. It rolled away and disappeared into the shadows.

Hawk watched helplessly. He'd found his axe again, but he didn't dare attack the vampire. Cold steel was no use against it. He needed a wooden stake. . . . He glared wildly about him, and his gaze fell on the coffin. A vampire must always return to its coffin before break of day. . . . Hawk grinned savagely as the answer came to him. He stepped forward, lifted his axe, and brought it swinging down onto the side of the coffin. The heavy wood split and splintered under the blow. Hawk jerked the blade free and struck again. The side sagged inwards, and splinters flew on the air. The vampire threw Fisher aside and darted forward. Hawk dropped his axe, grabbed the heaviest splinter from the coffin and buried it in the vampire's chest as the creature reached for him. For a moment they stood facing each other, the yellow eyes and grinning mouth only inches away from Hawk's face, and then the vampire suddenly collapsed and fell limply to the floor. It made surprised mewling sounds, and clutched at the thick wooden splinter protruding from its chest. Hawk threw himself down beside the vampire, snatched up his axe, and used the flat of the blade to hammer the splinter into the vampire's heart. It screamed and tore at him with its clawed hands, but he didn't care. He hit the wooden splinter again and again and again, driving it deep into the vampire's chest, and with every blow he struck he saw the dead girl's face as she hung from the butcher's hook. After a while he realised that the vampire had stopped struggling, and that Fisher was kneeling beside him.

"It's all right, Hawk. It's over."

He looked down at the vampire. The dirty yellow eyes stared sightlessly at the ceiling, and the clawed hands lay still at its sides. He raised his axe one last time, and cut savagely at the creature's neck. The steel blade sliced clean through and sank into the wooden floor beneath. The vampire seemed to collapse and fall in upon itself, and in a few seconds there was nothing left but dust. Hawk sighed slowly, pulled his axe out of the floor, and then sat back on his haunches. Some of the tension began to drain out of him. He looked wearily at Fisher, still kneeling beside him.

"You all right, lass?"

"I'll live."

Hawk smiled slightly. "Well, we got the vampire. Not exactly according to the book, but what the hell. You can't have everything."

He and Fisher rose painfully to their feet and leaned on each other a while until they felt strong enough to make their way back down the stairs. They left Trask and his daughter where they were. Burning the bodies could wait. Let the backup unit earn its pay for a change. Hawk and Fisher slowly made their way through the empty house and out into Chandler Lane. It was still hot and muggy, and the air stank of smoke and tannin, but after the house and what they'd found in it, the lane looked pretty good to them.

"You know," said Hawk reflectively, "there has to be an easier way to make a living."

2

Friends, Enemies and Politicians

At the house of the sorcerer called Gaunt, the party was just beginning. It was an old house, situated in one of the better parts of the city. The party was being held in the parlour, a comfortably large room that took up half the ground floor. The walls were lined with tall slender panels of beechwood, richly worked with carvings and motifs, and the ceiling boasted a single huge mural by one of Haven's most famous painters. But even without all that, Gaunt's parlour would have been impressive enough simply for its collection of priceless antique furniture. Chairs and tables and sideboards of an elegant simplicity mingled with the baroque styles of decades past. It was a tribute to the sorcerer's taste that the contrasting styles mixed so compatibly.

His parties were renowned throughout Haven; all the best people, wonderful food, and plenty of wine. Invitations were much coveted among the city Quality, but only rarely received. Since taking over the old DeFerrier house some four years earlier, the sorcerer Gaunt had shot up the social ladder with a speed that other newcomers could only envy. Not that Gaunt himself was in any way a snob. At his select affairs the elite of politics and business and society mixed freely, whatever their calling. But this evening the party was a strictly private affair, for a few friends. Councillor William Blackstone was celebrating his first year in office.

Blackstone was a large, heavyset man in his mid forties. Always well-groomed, polite and disarmingly easygoing, he had a politician's smile and a fanatic's heart. Blackstone was a reformer, and he had no time for compromise. He'd done more to clean up the city of Haven in his one year as Councillor than the rest of the Council put together. This made him very popular in the lower city, and earned him the undying enmity of the rich and powerful who made their living out of Haven's dark side. Unfortunately for those with a vested interest in other people's misery, Blackstone was himself quite wealthy, and not in the least averse to putting his money where his mouth was. At the end of his first year in office, the odds on his surviving a second year were being quoted as roughly four thousand to one. When Blackstone heard this he laughed, and bet a thousand in gold on himself.

His wife stood at his side as he talked animatedly with the sorcerer Gaunt about his next crusade, against the child prostitution rackets. Katherine Blackstone was a short, good-looking brunette in her mid twenties, and only slightly less feared than her husband. In her day she'd been one of the finest actresses ever to tread the boards in Haven, and though she'd put all that behind her on marrying Blackstone, she still possessed a mastery of words that left her enemies red-faced and floundering. Katherine had always had a gift for the barbed bon mot and the delicately judged put-down. She was also not averse to a little discreet character assassination when necessary.

Gaunt himself looked to be in his mid thirties, but was reputed to be much older. Tall, broad-shouldered but elegantly slim, he dressed always in sorcerer's black. The dark robes contrasted strongly with his pale, aquiline features. His voice was rich and commanding, and his pale grey eyes missed nothing. He shaved his head, but indulged himself with a pencil-thin moustache. He'd arrived in Haven from no-one-knew-where some four years ago, and immediately made a name for himself by single-handedly cleaning up the infamous Devil's Hook area.

Devil's Hook was a square mile of slums and alleyways backing onto the main docks, a breeding ground of poverty and despair. Men, women, and children worked appalling hours for meagre wages, and prices in the Hook were carefully controlled to keep the people permanently in debt. Those who spoke out against the conditions were openly intimidated and murdered. The city Guard avoided the Hook rather than risk a war with the gangs who ran it. And then the sorcerer Gaunt came to Haven. He walked into the Hook, unarmed, to see for himself what conditions were like. He walked out again some two hours later. Not long after, the Guard were called in to start the long business of carting away the dead bodies. Every member of every gang was dead. None of them had died easily.

The Hook held a celebration that lasted for over a week.

Certain businessmen tried to send new people into the Hook to start the various businesses up again, but Gaunt simply visited each man in turn and pointed out that any attempts to run sweatshops would be taken by him as a personal insult. Conditions within the Hook began to improve almost overnight.

Gaunt poured himself more wine, and savoured the bouquet.

"Darling, I don't know how you can drink that stuff,"

said Katherine Blackstone. "Hillsdown has some excellent orchards, but their grapes aren't worth the treading."

"I have no palate for wines," Gaunt admitted calmly. "But there's always been something about the Northern vintages that appeals to me. They're not particularly subtle, but there's no mistaking their power. If this wine was any stronger, it would leap out of the bottle and mug you. Would you care to try some, William?"

"Perhaps just a little," said Blackstone, grinning. "I had hoped it would get a little cooler once the sun went down, but I'm damned if I can tell the difference. Looks like it's going to be another long, dry summer." He gulped thirstily at the wine the sorcerer poured him, and nodded appreciatively.

Katherine tapped him gently on the arm. "You be careful with that stuff. You know you've no head for wine."

Blackstone nodded ruefully. "A grave drawback in a politician's life. Still, it has its bright side. Because I spend most of the evening with a glass of water in my hand, I'm still there listening when other people are getting flustered and careless."

"That's right," said Katherine sweetly. "Sometimes I'm surprised you don't go around taking notes."

"I have an excellent memory," said Blackstone.

"When it suits you," said Katherine.

"Now, now," said Gaunt quickly. "No quarrelling."

"Don't be silly, dear," said Katherine. "We enjoy it."

The three of them chuckled quietly together.

"So, William," said Gaunt. "How's your new bill going? Is the debate finally finished?"

"Looks that way," said Blackstone. "With a bit of luck, the bill should be made law by the end of the month. And not before time. Haven depends on its docks for most of its livelihood, and yet some of the owners have let them fall into a terrible state. Once my bill becomes law, those owners will be compelled to do something about renovating them, instead of just torching the older buildings for the insurance."

"Of course, the Council will help them out with grants for some of the work," said Katherine. "Just to sweeten the pot."

"One of your better ideas, that," said Blackstone.

"I'll be interested to see how it works out," said Gaunt. "Though I have a feeling it won't be that simple."

"Nothing ever is," said Blackstone.

"How's your latest project going, Gaunt?" asked Katherine. "Or aren't we allowed to ask?"

Gaunt shrugged. "It's no secret. I'm afraid I'm still not having much success. Truthspells are difficult things to put together. All the current versions produce nothing but the literal truth. They don't allow for nuances, half-truths and evasions. And then of course there's subjective truth and objective truth. . . ."

"Spare us, darling," protested Katherine, laughing. "You'd think I'd know enough by now not to enquire into a sorcerer's secrets. Magic must be the only thing in the world more complicated than politics."

"You obviously haven't had to spend half an evening listening to an old soldier talking about military tactics," said Blackstone dryly. "And speaking of which, aren't the Hightowers here yet? You did say they'd be coming."

"They'll be here," said Gaunt.

"Good," said Blackstone. "I want a word with Lord Hightower. He's supposed to be backing me on my next bill, but I haven't seen the man in almost a month. It wouldn't surprise me if he'd started getting cold feet."

"I shouldn't think so," said Gaunt. "Roderik's all right, when you get to know him. These old military types can be a bit of a bore when it comes to refighting all their old battles, but their word is their bond. If he's said he'll support you, he will. Count on it.''

"It's not his support I need so much as his money,'' said Blackstone dryly. ''Politicians can't live on applause alone, you know. The kind of campaigns I run are expensive. They need a constant flow of gold to keep them going, and even my resources aren't unlimited. Right now, Hightower's gold would come in very handy.''

"Mercenary,'' said Katherine affectionately.

At the other end of the huge parlour, Graham Dorimant and the witch called Visage were helping themselves to the fruit cordial in the silver punch bowl. As a refreshing fruit drink the cordial was something of a letdown, there being too much emphasis on the various powerful wines involved and not nearly enough on the fruit, but Dorimant was well known for drinking anything, provided he was thirsty enough. And the current heat wave had left him feeling very thirsty.

Graham Dorimant was medium height, late thirties, and somewhat overweight. He smiled frequently, and his dark eyes held an impartial warmth. He'd been Blackstone's political adviser for almost three years, and he was very good at his job. He had an encyclopaedic knowledge of Haven's electoral system, and he knew where the bodies were buried. Sometimes literally. He was on first-name terms with most of the Council, and quite a few of their staffs. He knew who could be persuaded, who could be browbeaten, and who could be bought. He knew when to talk and when to push, but most important of all, he had no political interests himself. Ideologies left him cold. He didn't give a damn one way or the other. He aided Blackstone simply because he admired the man. Dorimant himself was lazy, amoral, and uninterested in anything outside

Haven, but he nevertheless found much to admire in a man who was none of these things and yet attacked life with a zest Dorimant could only envy. Though he rarely admitted it to himself, Dorimant had found more fun and excitement in his time with Blackstone than at any other time in his life.

He drank thirstily at his fruit cordial, and smiled winningly at the witch Visage. Dorimant fancied himself a ladies' man and aspired to an elegance he was too lazy to fully bring off. He wore nothing but the finest and most fashionable clothes, but lacked the self-conscious élan of the true dandy. Basically, he had too much of a sense of humour to be able to take fashion seriously. His only real vanity was his hair. Although he'd just entered his late thirties, his hair was still jet black. There just wasn't as much of it as there used to be.

The witch Visage smiled back at Dorimant and sipped daintily at her drink. She was in her early twenties, with a great mass of wavy red hair that tumbled freely about her shoulders. Her skin was very pale, and her broad open face was dominated by her striking green eyes. There was a subtle wildness about her, like an animal from the Forest that had only recently been tamed. Men sensed the wildness and were attracted to it, but even the most insensitive knew instinctively that her constant slight smile hid very sharp teeth. Visage was tall for a woman, almost five foot nine, but painfully thin. She made Dorimant feel that he wanted to take her out to a restaurant and see that she had at least one good meal before he had his wicked way with her. Such a paternal, protective feeling was new to Dorimant, and he pushed it firmly to one side.

"Well, my dear," he said briskly, "how is our revered master? Your magics still keeping him safe and sound?"

"Of course," said Visage shyly, her voice as ever low

and demure. "As long as I am with him, no magic can harm him. And you, sir, does your advice protect his interests as well as I protect his health?"

"I try," smiled Dorimant. "Of course, a man as honest as William is bound to make enemies. He's too open and honest for his own good. If he would only agree to turn a blind eye now and again. . . ."

"He would not be the man he is, and neither of us would be interested in serving him. Am I not right?"

"As always, my dear," said Dorimant. "Would you care for some more cordial?"

"Thank you, I think I will. It is very close in here. Are you not having any more?"

"Perhaps later. I fear all this fruit is terribly fattening, and I must watch my waistline."

"That shouldn't be too difficult," said Visage sweetly. "There's enough of it."

Dorimant looked at her reproachfully.

Hawk and Fisher stood together before Gaunt's front door, waiting for someone to answer the bell. The sorcerer's house was a fair-sized two-storey building, standing in its own grounds, situated near the Eastern boundary of the city. A high wall surrounded the grounds, the old stonework mostly buried under a thick blanket of ivy. The grounds had been turned into a single massive garden, where strange herbs and unusual flowers grew in ornate patterns that were subtly disturbing to the eye. The night air was thick with the rich scent of a hundred mingled perfumes. Light from the full moon shimmered brightly on the single gravelled path. The house itself had no particular character. It stood simply and squarely where it had stood for hundreds of years, and though the stonework was discolored by wind and rain and the passing of years, its very simplicity suggested a strength that would maintain the house for years to come.

The front door was large and solid, and Hawk eyed the bell pull dubiously, wondering if he should try it again in case it hadn't worked the first time. He tugged impatiently at his high collar and shifted his weight from foot to foot. Both he and Fisher were wearing the formal Guards' uniform of navy blue and gold, topped with their best black cloaks. The heavy clothes were stiff, uncomfortable, and very hot. Hawk and Fisher had protested loudly before they set out, but to no avail. Guards had to look their best when mixing with High Society. To do otherwise would reflect badly on the Guards. Hawk and Fisher had given in. Eventually.

"Leave your collar alone," said Fisher. "You're not doing it any good."

"I hate formal clothes," growled Hawk. "Why did we have to draw this damned duty? I thought that after staking a vampire we'd have been entitled to a little time off at least, but no; just time for a quick healing spell, and off we go again."

Fisher chuckled dryly. "Nothing succeeds like success. We solved the vampire case where everyone else had failed, so naturally we get handed the next most difficult case, bodyguarding Blackstone."

Hawk shook his head dolefully. "The only really honest Councillor in the city. No wonder so many people want him dead."

"You ever meet him?" asked Fisher.

"Shook his hand once, at an election rally."

"Did you vote for him?"

"Well, the other guy was handing out money."

Fisher laughed. "An honest Guard; you stayed bought."

Hawk smiled. "Like hell. I took their money, voted for

Blackstone anyway, and defied them to do anything about it. It didn't exactly make their day.'' He grinned broadly, remembering.

"I admire Blackstone's courage," said Fisher, "if not his good sense. Standing up against all the vested interests in this city takes real guts. We could do a lot more in our job if half our superiors weren't openly corrupt."

Hawk grunted, and pulled at his collar again. "What do you know about this sorcerer, Gaunt?"

"Not much. Fairly powerful, as sorcerers go, but he's not flashy about it. Likes to throw parties, but otherwise keeps himself to himself. Not married, and doesn't chase women. Or men, for that matter. No one knows where he came from originally, but rumour has it he was once sorcerer to the King. Then he left the Court under something of a cloud, and came and settled here in Haven. Made a name for himself in the Hook. You remember that?"

"Yeah," said Hawk. "I was part of the team that had to go in there and clean up the mess. We were still carrying out the bodies a week later."

"That's right," said Fisher. "I was still working on the Shattered Bullion case." She looked at Hawk thoughtfully. "You never told me about this before. Was it bad? I heard stories. . . ."

"It was bad," said Hawk. "There were no survivors among the gangs—no wounded, no dying; only the dead. We still don't know what killed them, but it wasn't very neat. Most of the bodies had been ripped apart. There's no doubt the gangs were evil. They did some terrible things. But what happened to them was worse."

"And this is the man whose party we're attending as bodyguards," said Fisher, grimacing. "Great. Just great."

She broke off as the front door swung suddenly open. A bright, cheerful light filled the hall beyond and spilled out into the night. Hawk and Fisher blinked uncertainly as their eyes adjusted to the glare, and then they bowed politely to the man standing before them. Gaunt took in their Guards' cloaks, and inclined his head slightly in return.

"William's bodyguards. Do come in; I've been expecting you."

He stepped back a pace and waited patiently as they made their way past him into the hall. He shut the door carefully and turned back to extend a slender, well-manicured hand. Hawk shook it firmly, and then gritted his teeth as Gaunt all but crushed his fingers in a powerful grip. He hated people who did that. Somehow he kept his polite smile in place, and then surreptitiously flexed his fingers as Gaunt turned to Fisher. The sorcerer took Fisher's hand and raised it to his lips. Hawk frowned slightly. He wasn't too keen on people who did that, either. Fisher smiled politely at the sorcerer. He wasn't quite what she'd expected. After Hawk's tale of what he'd found in the Hook, she'd been expecting someone more . . . impressive. With his mild grey eyes and pleasant smile, Gaunt just didn't look the part.

The sorcerer looked at the two Guards thoughtfully. "Captain Hawk and Captain Fisher," he said, after a moment. "I've heard of you."

"Nothing good, I hope," said Fisher, and Gaunt chuckled.

"You did an excellent job of taking care of the Chandler Lane vampire. Most impressive."

Hawk raised an eyebrow. "News travels fast in Haven."

Gaunt smiled. "I have my sources."

"Yeah," said Hawk. "I'll just bet you do."

"If you'll follow me," said the sorcerer politely.

"Councillor Blackstone is already here, with some of my other guests."

He led the way down the hall to a heavy oaken door on the right. He pushed it open, and then stood back to usher the two Guards into the parlour. The guests looked briefly at Hawk and Fisher, took in the black cloaks, and went back to their conversations. Hawk looked casually about him, getting the feel of the place. Two huge windows were blocked off by closed wooden shutters, despite the heat. There was only the one door, leading into the hall. Hawk relaxed a little. If push came to shove, it shouldn't be too difficult to defend the parlour against an attack. Assuming anyone was suicidal enough to take on the sorcerer Gaunt in his own home.

Gaunt went over to Blackstone and spoke quietly to him. Blackstone glanced at Hawk and Fisher, excused himself to the witch Visage, and walked back with Gaunt to meet them. He shook them both by the hand; the usual quick, firm handshake of the seasoned politician.

"Glad you're both here," he said briskly. "I'm sure I'll feel a lot safer with you two at my side. It's only for the next few days, until my bill has become law. After that, the danger will be over."

"Really?" said Fisher. "The way I hear it, you've got more enemies in Haven than the Chancellor on tax day."

Blackstone laughed. "Well, the immediate danger, anyway. If I'd wanted a safe occupation, I wouldn't have entered politics."

"Well then, Councillor," said Hawk briskly, "what would you like us to do?"

"For tonight, just mingle with the guests and enjoy yourselves," said Blackstone pleasantly. "I'm in no danger here, not in Gaunt's house. Even my enemies know better than to risk his anger."

"You are always safe here, William," said Gaunt quietly. "This house is protected against any and all intrusions."

"And now, if you'll excuse us," said Blackstone, flashing a quick smile at Hawk and Fisher, "Gaunt and I have some business to discuss. Do help yourself to a drink and something to eat."

The politician and the sorcerer moved away, talking animatedly. Hawk and Fisher looked at each other.

"Free booze," said Fisher. "This may not be such a bad assignment after all."

"Yeah," said Hawk.

They made their way over to the punch bowl and helped themselves to the fruit cordial. Hawk wrinkled his nose at the taste, but drank it anyway. The room was hot, he was thirsty, and besides, it was free. Various canapés had been laid out beside the punch bowl, arranged in interesting patterns in the mistaken belief that this would make the food appear more appetising. Hawk didn't even recognise half of it, but he tried one anyway, just to show himself willing.

"Not bad," he said indistinctly.

"I'm glad you think so," said Katherine Blackstone. "Gaunt prides himself on his culinary skills."

Hawk chewed and swallowed quickly to empty his mouth as the Councillor's wife looked him and Fisher over. She seemed friendly enough, in a condescending way. Katherine's gaze lingered on Hawk more than Fisher, and he wondered if he'd imagined the sudden glitter in her eyes. The way she was acting, he half expected her to lean forward and pin a rosette on him.

"So you're the best the Guard could supply," said Katherine finally. "I do hope you're as fearsome as your reputation suggests."

"We try," said Hawk.

Katherine looked thoughtfully at his face. "The scars are certainly impressive, darling. What happened to your eye?"

"I lost it in a card game."

Katherine gave him a startled look, and then dissolved into giggles. It made her look much younger. "My dear, I think you won that one on points. Do help yourself to the spiced lamb; it's really quite delicious. I believe there's even some asparagus, though where Gaunt managed to get it at this time of the year is beyond me. Knowing a sorcerer does have its advantages, I suppose."

There was a pause, while they all busied themselves with the food. Fisher smiled suddenly as she bit into a piece of cold garlic sausage.

"We could have used some of this earlier today."

"What?" said Katherine. "Oh, the garlic. Gaunt was just telling us about the vampire before you arrived. Horrible creatures. Did you really kill it by driving a wooden stake through its heart?"

"Eventually," said Hawk.

"Such a pity about Trask," said Katherine. "I mean, he wasn't much of a Councillor, but he did a good enough job, and at least you knew where you were with him. And his was a marginal seat, you know. Now there'll have to be another election, and I hate to think who we might get in his place. Better the devil you know, and all that."

Hawk and Fisher nodded politely and said nothing. They hadn't told anyone about Trask being the vampire's Judas Goat. They just passed him off as another victim, along with his daughter. It was true enough, in a way. And besides, his widow was going to have a hard enough time as it was. Katherine Blackstone chattered on for a while, talking lightly about this and that, and then fluttered away to talk to Graham Dorimant. Hawk looked at Fisher.

"Well?" he said dryly. "What did you make of that?"

"Beats me," said Fisher. "Katherine Blackstone, coming on like an empty-headed socialite? That's not the woman I've heard so much about."

"Maybe it's a test of some kind. Checking us out to see if we're smart enough to see through the act."

Fisher scowled dubiously. "Could be, I suppose."

"Actually, it's a little more complicated than that," said the witch Visage.

Hawk and Fisher turned quickly to find her standing beside them. Hawk's hand dropped to his axe. He hadn't heard her approaching. . . . Visage saw the movement, and smiled slightly.

"I'm not your enemy, Captain Hawk. In fact, I'm glad you're here. I've had a premonition about William."

Hawk and Fisher looked quickly at each other, and then back at the slender redhead before them.

"A premonition," said Hawk slowly. "You think he's in danger?"

"Yes. I'm Visage. I'm a witch. It's my job to protect William from magical threats. He should be safe enough here in Gaunt's house. I've never seen so many defensive spells. The place is crawling with them. And yet . . . there's a feeling in the air. It worries me. I've given William some extra protection, but still . . ."

"Have you sensed anything in particular?" asked Fisher quietly.

Visage shook her head, frowning. "Nothing definite. Somebody here, or close by, is planning a death; and the victim is either William or someone connected with him. That's all I can get."

"Have you told Blackstone?" asked Hawk.

"Of course. He isn't taking the threat seriously enough."

"Somebody here or close by," said Fisher. "Maybe we should check the grounds."

"I suggested that to Gaunt," said Visage. "He said no one could get into the grounds or the house without his knowing." She looked at Hawk steadily. "Unless you do something to stop it, someone is going to die in this house. Tonight."

She turned suddenly and walked away. Hawk and Fisher watched her go.

"Great start to the party," said Hawk.

"Isn't it," said Fisher.

"Did you notice," said Hawk thoughtfully, "that she never did get around to explaining why Katherine Blackstone was acting out of character?"

"Yeah," said Fisher. "Interesting, that."

They looked at each other a moment, shrugged, and helped themselves to more of the fruit cordial.

"Who the hell would be desperate enough to attack Blackstone in Gaunt's house?" said Hawk. "All right, Gaunt isn't the most powerful sorcerer I've ever met, but I'd put him right up there in the top ten. I certainly wouldn't cross him without a damn good reason."

"Right," said Fisher. "If nothing else, our potential murderer must be pretty damn confident. Or crazy. Or both."

"Or he knows something we don't." Hawk scowled grimly. "Think we should say something to Blackstone?"

"Not yet," said Fisher "What could we tell him that he doesn't already know? Besides, like you said, who could get to him here?"

"There's no place so well-defended that someone determined enough can't find a way in," said Hawk firmly.

"After all, it might not be a direct attack. It could be something that's been planned in advance."

Fisher nodded slowly. "A prearranged spell, or curse. Or maybe they poisoned the food."

"Or the drink," said Hawk.

They looked at their empty glasses.

"Unlikely," said Fisher. "The witch said someone was planning *a* death tonight, not several. And anyway, Gaunt would surely be able to detect the presence of anything poisonous. Same for any spells."

"I suppose so," said Hawk. "All right, poison is out. But a direct attack seems even more unlikely. In order to get to Blackstone, an assassin would have to get past all of Gaunt's defences, and then fight his way past us. There are assassins that good in the Low Kingdoms, but I don't really think Blackstone's important enough to warrant their attentions. No, I think a magical attack of some kind has to be the most likely."

"But according to the witch, this house is covered with defensive spells."

"Yeah." Hawk shook his head disgustedly. "Nothing's ever simple, is it? You know, Isobel, just once I think I'd like to work on a case that was simple and straightforward. Just for a change."

"So what are we going to do?" asked Fisher.

"Stay close to Blackstone, and watch everyone else very closely."

"Sounds like an excellent idea," said Dorimant.

Hawk and Fisher looked him over coldly, and Dorimant didn't miss the way their hands fell naturally to the weapons at their sides. He felt a sudden chill run down his spine. As a political adviser, Dorimant had mixed with some hard people in his time, but one look into Hawk's cold eye was enough to convince him that everything he'd heard about Hawk and Fisher was true. These people were dangerous. He smiled at them calmly, and hoped they'd put the sweat on his brow down to the heat.

"Allow me to introduce myself. Graham Dorimant, William's political adviser."

Hawk nodded politely. "I'm . . ."

"Oh, I know who you two are," said Dorimant quickly. "Everyone in Haven's heard of Hawk and Fisher."

"Fame at last," said Fisher dryly.

Dorimant chuckled. "Honest Guards are as rare as honest politicians. That's why I particularly asked for you as William's bodyguards."

"The witch says that Blackstone is in danger," said Fisher bluntly. "She thinks that someone's going to try and kill him tonight."

Dorimant frowned. "I wouldn't take Visage too seriously, Captain Fisher. She's good enough at her job, but she sees threats in every shadow."

"But Blackstone does have enemies," said Hawk.

"Oh, certainly. What politician doesn't? And William's policies aren't exactly aimed at making him popular with the vested interests who make this city the cesspool it is. But when all is said and done, he's safe here. Gaunt was telling me about some of his defences earlier, and I can assure you that nothing and nobody gets into this house unless Gaunt says so. Believe me, William has absolutely nothing to worry about tonight."

"Unless one of his guests turns out to be an assassin," said Fisher.

Dorimant looked at her sharply. "Captain Fisher, everyone at this party is a friend of William's, and has been for years. Not one of them has anything to gain by his death. The only people at this party that I can't personally vouch for are you and Captain Hawk. And your reputations suggest you lack the taste for assassination work.''

"Yeah," said Hawk. "The pay's good, but the working conditions are lousy.''

Fisher nodded solemnly. Dorimant looked from one to the other, and then smiled reluctantly.

"Captain Hawk, Captain Fisher, right now William's under a lot of pressure. His political opponents are doing their best to sabotage his new bill, and there have been a few death threats. Usual anonymous rubbish. I thought having you two around for the next few days might make him feel a little more secure. All you have to do is stick with him, and don't let anyone within arm's reach of him unless I vouch for them. All right?''

"Sure," said Hawk. "I've done bodyguarding work before.''

"Good," said Dorimant. "You do know you'll be staying the night here, along with the rest of us?''

"Yeah," said Fisher. "We didn't have time to pack a bag, but no doubt Gaunt can provide us with what we need.''

"Of course," said Dorimant. "I'll have a word with him.''

The doorbell rang, and Gaunt went into the hall to answer it. Hawk frowned slightly.

"Why does a great sorcerer like Gaunt answer his own door? Doesn't he have any servants?''

Dorimant smiled. "Gaunt doesn't trust servants. Afraid they might be after his secrets, I suppose. Industrial espionage is rife among magicians.''

"Secrets," said Fisher. "What do you know about Gaunt, sir Dorimant?''

"Not much. He's a private man. William knows him better than I do. There are rumours he used to be sorcerer to the King, until they had a falling out. The rumours don't say what they might have argued about. Gaunt's a quiet sort, usually. Don't think I've ever known him to raise his voice in anger. On the other hand, you know what he did in the Hook. . . ."

"Yeah." Fisher scowled, her hand idly caressing the pommel of her sword. "I don't trust sorcerers."

"Not many people do," said Dorimant dryly. "But Gaunt is no threat to William. They've been friends for years."

He broke off as Gaunt came back into the parlour, accompanied by a tall, wiry man in his late twenties. He had a shock of long dark hair and a thick curly beard, so that most of his face was hidden from casual view. He smiled easily, but the smile didn't reach his eyes. He was dressed in the latest fashion, and wore it well. Considering that the latest fashion included tightly cut trousers and a padded jerkin with a chin-high collar, this was no mean achievement. It would have been easy to dismiss him as a dandy, if it hadn't been for the sword that hung at his left hip, in a well-worn scabbard. Blackstone and his wife went over to greet the newcomer.

"Now there's a man you can distrust," said Dorimant quietly. "Edward Bowman. William's right-hand man. A brilliant politician with a first-class mind. Watch him. The man's a rat."

Hawk frowned, and started to ask him more, but Dorimant was already walking away, heading back to the witch Visage. Hawk looked back at Bowman. Gaunt and Blackstone were deep in conversation, leaving Katherine chatting with Bowman. Hawk's eye narrowed as he watched them. There was nothing specific he could put his finger on, but there was something about the way Katherine and Bowman were talking together. . . . They were *too* friendly. They smiled too much, their concentration was too intense, and they touched each other politely but too often.

"Yeah," said Fisher. "They're certainly glad to see each other, aren't they?"

"Probably just good friends," said Hawk.

"Sure. Sure."

The doorbell sounded again, and Gaunt disappeared into the hall. Blackstone moved over to join Bowman and Katherine. Hawk watched closely, but couldn't see any obvious signs of tension between them. They all smiled a little too brightly and too often, but then, they were politicians. . . . Hawk sighed, and looked away.

"I assume the bell means more guests," he said tiredly. "That's all we need; more suspects to watch."

"You worry too much," said Fisher, pouring herself more of the fruit cordial. "Look, all we've got to do is keep the man alive for the next three days until his bill becomes law. After that, the pressure will be off, and he won't need us anymore. Surely we can keep him out of trouble for three days."

Hawk shrugged, unconvinced. "I don't like coming onto a case unprepared. We don't know enough about what's going on here, and we certainly don't know enough about the people involved. Katherine Blackstone is acting out of character. Visage knows why, but won't tell us. Instead, she tells us that Councillor Blackstone is in danger, in one of the best defended houses in the city. Blackstone's political adviser warns us about Blackstone's right-hand man, who turns out to be very friendly with the Councillor's wife. I've got a bad feeling about this, Isobel."

"You're always getting bad feelings."

"And I'm usually right."

Fisher chuckled affectionately. "We've had a long hard day, my love. It's just the tiredness talking, that's all. Blackstone is perfectly safe here. We're just window dressing. Now, have a drink, and relax a little. Okay?"

"Okay." Hawk smiled fondly at Fisher. "You were always the sensible one. What would I do without you, lass?"

"Beats the hell out of me," said Fisher, smiling. "Now, relax. Everything's going to be fine."

Gaunt came back into the parlour, and Hawk's heart sank. He knew the middle-aged couple with the sorcerer only too well. Lord and Lady Hightower were a prominent part of Haven's High Society. They moved in all the right circles, and knew all the right people. In a very real sense, they were part of the moneyed and influential elite who controlled Haven. They were also, surprisingly, two of Blackstone's strongest supporters.

Lord Roderik Hightower was a stocky, medium-height man in his early fifties. His short-cropped hair was iron grey, and his piercing dark eyes stared unyieldingly from a harsh, weatherbeaten face. Only a few years earlier, he'd been the Chief Commander of the Low Kingdoms' army, and a legend in his own lifetime. He always led his men into battle, and he was always the last to retreat. His grasp of strategy was second to none, and he had guts of solid steel. A soldier's soldier. He was still solidly muscled, but signs of wear were finally beginning to show. He was getting slower, and old wounds gnawed at him when it rained. He'd retired from the army rather than accept the desk job they offered him, and had immediately looked for a new challenge with which to occupy himself. He finally settled on politics, and took on the campaign to clean up Haven with the same determination and gusto he'd shown in his army days.

Hawk knew him from a year or so back. There had been a series of werewolf murders on the lower Northside, and Hawk had been one of the investigating Guards. It had been a complicated, messy case. Hawk had finally identified the shapechanger and destroyed it, but not before three more men had been killed. One of them was Hightower's only son. Hawk's superiors had stood by him, but Hightower still blamed him for his son's death.

Great, thought Hawk. *Just what I needed. More complications.*

He looked curiously at Hightower's wife, the Lady Elaine. A very well-preserved early fifties, she wore the latest fashion with style and dignity. Her dress was long and flowing, despite the muggy weather, and studded with semiprecious stones. She fanned herself constantly with an intricately painted paper fan, but otherwise seemed unaffected by the heat. She had a long mane of pure white hair and showed it off to advantage. Her face had a strong bone structure, and she was still stunningly good-looking, despite her years. All in all, she looked splendid, and she knew it. She held her husband's arm protectively, and looked around Gaunt's parlour with such poise that she seemed to be suggesting that simply by entering such a room she was most definitely slumming.

Hawk felt an almost overwhelming urge to sneak up behind her and kick her in the bustle.

Fisher leaned closer to Hawk. "Hightower . . ." she said softly. "Wasn't he the one who . . ."

"Yeah," said Hawk.

"Maybe he's forgotten by now."

"I doubt it."

Hightower looked across the room, saw Hawk and Fisher, and stiffened slightly. He spoke quietly to his wife, who looked at the two Guards as though they'd just crawled out from under a rock. She reluctantly let go of her husband's arm and moved away to greet Blackstone. Lord Hightower glared at Hawk for a long moment, and then walked slowly across the length of the room to confront him. Hawk and Fisher bowed politely. Hightower didn't bow in return. He waited for Hawk to straighten up, and then studied him coldly.

"So. You're William's bodyguards."

"That's right, my Lord," said Hawk.

"I should have had you drummed out of the Guard when I had the chance."

"You tried hard enough, my Lord," said Hawk calmly. "Luckily my superiors knew the facts of the matter. Your son's death was a tragic accident."

"He'd still be alive if you'd done your job properly!"

"Perhaps. I did my best, my Lord."

Hightower sniffed, and looked disparagingly at Fisher. "This is your woman, is it?"

"This is my partner and my wife," said Hawk. "Captain Fisher."

"And if you raise your voice to my husband again," said Fisher calmly, "I'll knock you flat on your arse, right here and now."

Hightower flushed angrily, and started to splutter a reply. And then his voice died away as he looked into Fisher's steady eyes and saw that she meant it. Hightower had a lifetime's experience of fighting men, and knew without a shadow of a doubt that Fisher would kill him if she thought he was a threat to her husband. He recalled some of the things he'd heard about Hawk and Fisher, and suddenly they didn't seem quite so impossible after all. He sniffed again, turned his back on the two Guards, and walked back to his wife with as much dignity as he could muster.

"How to make friends and influence people," said Hawk.

"To hell with him," said Fisher. "Anyone who wants to take you on has to go through me first."

Hawk smiled at her fondly. "I knew there had to be some reason why I put up with you." His smile faded away. "I liked Hightower's son. He hadn't been in the Guard long, but he meant well, and he tried so hard. He was just in the wrong place at the wrong time, and he died because of it."

"What happened on that werewolf case?" said Fisher. "That's another one you never told me much about."

"Not much to tell. The case started badly and went downhill fast. We didn't have much to go on, and what little we thought we knew about werewolves turned out to be mostly untrue. According to legend, the werewolf in human shape is excessively hairy, has two fingers the same length, and has a pentacle on his palm. Rubbish, all of it. Also according to the legend, the man takes on his wolf shape when the full moon rises, and only turns back again when the moon goes down. Our shapechanger could turn from man to wolf and back again whenever he felt like it, as long as the full moon was up. That made finding him rather difficult. We got him eventually. Ordinary-looking guy. You could walk right past him in the street and never notice him. I killed him with a silver sword. He lay on the ground with the blood running out of him, and cried, as though he couldn't understand why any of this was happening to him. He hadn't wanted to kill anyone; the werewolf curse made him do it. He hadn't wanted to die either, and at the end he cried like a small child that's been punished and doesn't know why."

Fisher put an arm across his shoulders and hugged him.

"How very touching," said an amused voice. Hawk

and Fisher looked round to see Edward Bowman standing to their right, smiling sardonically. Fisher moved unhurriedly away from Hawk. Bowman put out his hand, and Hawk shook it warily. Like Blackstone, Bowman had a politician's quick and impersonal handshake. He shook Fisher's hand too.

"Enjoying the party?" he asked, smiling impartially at Hawk and Fisher.

"It has its ups and downs," said Hawk dryly.

"Ah yes," said Bowman. "I saw you and Hightower. Unfortunate business about his son. You'd do well to be wary of Hightower, Captain Hawk. The Lord Roderik is well known for his ability to hold a grudge."

"What's his connection with Blackstone?" asked Fisher. "I'd have thought a man like Hightower, old army and High Society, would be conservative by nature, rather than a reformer."

Bowman smiled knowingly. "Normally you'd be right; and thereby hangs a tale. Up until a few years ago, Lord Roderik was a devoted advocate of the status quo. Change could only be for the worse, and those who actually lobbied for reforms were nothing but malcontents and traitors. And then the King summoned Lord Hightower to Court, and told him it had been decided by the Assembly that he was too old to lead the army anymore, and he would have to step down to make way for a younger man. According to my spies at Court, Hightower just stood there and looked at the King like he couldn't believe his ears. Apparently he hadn't thought the mandatory retirement from the field at fifty would apply to someone as important as him. The King was very polite about it, even offered Hightower a position as his personal military adviser, but Hightower wouldn't have any of it. If he couldn't be a real soldier, he'd resign his commission. I don't think he really believed they'd go that far. Until they did.

"He was never the same after that. Thirty years of his life given to the army, and he didn't even get a pension, because he resigned. Not that he needed a pension, of course, but it was the principle of the thing. He came back here, to his home and his family, but couldn't seem to settle down. Tried to offer his advice and expertise to the Council, but they didn't want to know. I think he joined up with Blackstone originally just to spite them. Told you he carried grudges. Then he discovered Reform, and he's been unbearable ever since. There's no one more fanatical than a convert to a Cause. Still, there's no denying he's been very useful to us. His name opens quite a few doors in Haven."

"It should," said Hawk. "His family owns a fair chunk of it. And his wife's family is one of the oldest in the city." He looked thoughtfully at Bowman. "How did you get involved with Blackstone?"

Bowman shrugged. "I liked his style. He was one of the few politicians I met who actually seemed interested in doing something to improve the lives of the people who live in this rat hole of a city. I've been in politics all my life; my father was a Councillor till the day he died, but I hadn't really been getting anywhere. It's not enough in politics to have a good mind and good intentions; you have to have a good personal image as well. I've never had much talent for being popular, but William has. I knew he was going places from the first day I met him. But, at that time, he didn't have any experience. He threw away chances, because he didn't even know they were there. So, we decided to work together. I provided the experience, he provided the style. It hasn't worked out too badly. We get on well together, and we get things done."

"And he gets all the power, and all the credit," said Fisher.

"I'm not ambitious," said Bowman. "And there's more to life than credit."

"Indeed there is," said Katherine Blackstone. She moved in to stand beside Bowman, and Hawk and Fisher didn't miss the way they stood together.

"Tell me," said Katherine, sipping daintily at her drink, "where did you and your wife come from originally, Captain Hawk? I'm afraid I can't quite place your accent."

"We're from the North," said Hawk vaguely. "Up around Hillsdown."

"Hillsdown," said Katherine thoughtfully. "That's a monarchy, isn't it?"

"More or less," said Fisher.

"The Low Kingdoms must seem rather strange to you," said Bowman. "I don't suppose democracy has worked its way up North yet."

"Not yet," said Hawk. "The world's a big place, and change travels slowly. When I discovered the Low Kingdoms were in fact governed by an elected Assembly, presided over by a constitutional monarch with only limited powers, it was as though my whole world had been tipped upside down. How could he be King if he didn't rule? But the idea; the idea that every man and woman should have a say in how the country should be run: that was staggering. There's no denying the system does have its drawbacks, and I've seen most of them right here in Haven, but it has its attractions too."

"It's the way of the future," said Bowman.

"You might just be right," said Hawk.

The doorbell rang, and Gaunt went off to answer it. Bowman and Katherine chatted a while longer about nothing in particular, and then moved away to talk quietly with each other. Fisher looked after them thoughtfully.

"I don't trust Bowman; he smiles too much."

Hawk shrugged. "That's his job; he's a politician, remember? But did you see the way Katherine's face lit up every time Bowman looked at her?"

"Yeah," said Fisher, grinning. "There's definitely something going on there."

"Scandalmonger," said Hawk.

"Not at all," said Fisher. "I'm just romantic, that's all."

Gaunt came back into the parlour with a tall, muscular man in his late forties. Hawk took one look at the new arrival and nearly spilled his drink. Standing beside Gaunt was Adam Stalker, possibly the most renowned hero ever to come out of the Low Kingdoms. In his time he'd fought every monster you could think of, and then some. He'd single-handedly toppled the evil Baron Cade from his mountain fortress, and freed hundreds of prisoners from the foul dungeons under Cade's Keep. He'd been the confidant of kings and the champion of the oppressed. He'd served in a dozen armies, in this cause and that, bringing aid and succour to those who had none. His feats of daring and heroism had spread across the known world, and were the subject of countless songs and stories. Adam Stalker: demonslayer and hero.

He stood a head and shoulders taller than anyone else in the room, and was almost twice as wide as some of them. His shoulder-length black hair was shot with grey now, but he was still an impressive and powerful figure. His clothes were simple but elegantly cut. He looked around the room like a soldier gazing across a battlefield, nodding at the familiar faces, and then his cold blue eyes fell on Hawk and Fisher. He strode quickly over to them, crushed Hawk's hand in his, and clapped him on the back. Hawk staggered under the blow.

"I heard about your run-in with the Chandler Lane vampire," Stalker said gruffly. "You did a good job, Captain Hawk. A damned good job."

"Thanks," said Hawk, just a little breathlessly. "My partner helped."

"Of course." Stalker nodded briefly to Fisher. "Well done, my dear." He looked back at Hawk. "I've heard good things about you, Hawk. This city has much to thank you for."

"Yeah," said Fisher. "We're thinking of putting in for a raise."

"Thank you, sir warrior," said Hawk quickly. "We do our best, but I'm sure we've a long way to go before we become as renowned as Adam Stalker."

Stalker smiled and waved a hand dismissively. "Minstrels exaggerate. I take it you're here as William's bodyguards. You shouldn't have any trouble, not with me and Gaunt to look after him. Still, I can always use a backup. I'll talk to you again later; I want to hear all about this vampire killing. I once stumbled across a whole nest of the things, up in the Broken Crag range. Nasty business."

He nodded briskly, and strode off to speak to Blackstone. Hawk and Fisher watched him go.

"Big, isn't he?" said Hawk.

"I'll say," said Fisher. "He must be close on seven feet tall. And did you see the size of those muscles?"

"Yeah." Hawk looked at her narrowly. "You were a bit short with him, weren't you?"

"He was a bit short with me. He's obviously one of those men who think women should stay at home while the men go out to be heroes. You ever met him before, Hawk?"

"No. Heard most of the songs, though. If only half of them are true, he's a remarkable man. I wasn't sure I believed some of the stories, but now I've met him . . . I don't know. He's certainly impressive."

"Right." Fisher sipped thoughtfully at her drink. "A very dangerous man, if crossed."

Hawk looked at her sharply. "Oh, come on. Stalker as an assassin? That's ridiculous. What reason could a great hero like Stalker possibly have for taking on a small-time politician like Blackstone? We're talking about a man who's supposed to have toppled kings in his time."

Fisher shrugged. "I don't know. He just strikes me as a little too good to be true, that's all."

"You're just jealous because he congratulated me, and not you."

Fisher laughed, and emptied her glass. "Maybe."

"How many of those have you had?" asked Hawk suddenly.

"Two or three. I'm thirsty."

"Then ask for a glass of water. This is no time to be getting legless. Hightower would just love to find some reason to drop us in it."

"Spoilsport." Fisher put down her empty glass and looked about her. The party seemed to be livening up. The chatter of raised voices filled the parlour, along with a certain amount of self-satisfied laughter. Every hand held a wineglass, and the first few bottles were already empty.

Hawk moved away to talk to Blackstone about the security arrangements, and Fisher was left on her own. She looked disinterestedly around her. Society gatherings didn't appeal to her much. Private jokes, malicious gossip, and sugary wines were no substitute for good food and ale in the company of friends. Not that she was particularly fond of that kind of gathering, either. *I guess I'm just basically antisocial,* thought Fisher sardonically. She shrugged and smiled, and then stood up a little straighter as Edward Bowman came over to stand before her. She bowed politely, and he nodded briefly in return.

"Captain Fisher. All alone?"

"For the moment."

"Now that is unacceptable; a good-looking woman like yourself should never want for company."

Fisher raised a mental eyebrow. Her face was striking rather than pretty, and she knew it. *He's after something. . . .*

"I'm not very fond of company," she said carefully.

"Don't much care for crowds myself," said Bowman, smiling engagingly. "Why don't we go somewhere more private, just the two of us?"

"I don't think Gaunt would like that. We are his guests. And after all, I'm here to do a job."

"Gaunt won't say anything." Bowman leaned closer, his voice dropping to a murmur. "No one will say anything. I'm an important man, my dear."

Fisher looked him straight in the eye. "You don't believe in wasting time, do you?"

Bowman shrugged. "Life is short. Why are we still talking? There are so many other, more pleasurable things we could be doing."

"I don't think so," said Fisher calmly.

"What?" Bowman looked at her sharply. "I don't think you understand, my dear. No one turns me down. No one."

Fisher smiled coldly. "Want to bet?"

Bowman scowled, all the amiability gone from his face as though it had never been there. "You forget your place, Captain. I have friends among your superior officers. All I have to do is drop a word in the right quarter. . . ."

"You'd really do that?"

"Believe it, Captain. I can ruin your career, have you thrown in jail. . . . You'd be surprised what can happen to you. Unless, of course . . ."

He reached out a hand towards her, and then stopped suddenly and looked down. Fisher had a dagger in her left hand, the point pressed against his stomach. Bowman stood very still.

"You threaten me again," said Fisher quietly, "and I'll cut you one you'll carry for the rest of your days. And be grateful my husband hasn't noticed anything. He'd kill you on the spot, and damn the consequences. Now go away, and stay away. Understand?"

Bowman nodded jerkily, and Fisher made the dagger disappear. Bowman turned and walked away. Fisher leaned back against the buffet table and shook her head resignedly.

I think I preferred the party when it was boring. . . .

Gaunt stood alone by the doorway, keeping a careful eye on the time. The first course would be ready soon, and he didn't want it to be overdone. The first course set the mood for the meal to come. He looked around at his guests, and then winced slightly as he saw Stalker making his way determinedly towards him. Gaunt sighed, and bowed politely to Stalker. The giant warrior inclined his head briefly in response.

"I'd like a word with you, sir sorcerer."

"Of course, Adam. What can I do for you?"

"Sell me this house."

Gaunt shook his head firmly. "Adam, I've told you before; I'm not interested in selling. This house suits me very well, and I've spent a great deal of time investing both it and the grounds with my own magical protections. Moving now would be not only expensive and highly inconvenient, it would also mean at least six months' hard work removing those spells before anyone else could live here.''

''The money needn't be a problem,'' said Stalker. ''I'm a rich man these days. You can name your price, sorcerer.''

''It's not a question of money, Adam. This house suits me. I'm quite happy here and I don't want to move. Now I hate to be ungracious about this, but there's really no point in your continuing to pester me about selling. Your gold doesn't tempt me in the least; I already have all I need. I don't see why this house is so important to you, Adam. There are others just like it scattered all over the city. Why are you so obsessed with mine?''

''Personal reasons,'' said Stalker shortly. ''If you should happen to change your mind, perhaps you would give me first refusal.''

''Of course, Adam. Now, while you're here, I'd like a word with you.''

''Yes?''

''What's happened between you and William? Have you quarrelled?''

''No.'' Stalker looked steadily at Gaunt. ''Why do you ask?''

''Oh, come on, Adam; I'm not blind. I don't think the pair of you have exchanged two words you didn't have to in the last few weeks. I thought perhaps you'd had a falling-out, or something.''

Stalker shook his head. ''Not really. I'm here, aren't I? It was just a difference of opinion over what our next project should be. It'll work itself out. And now, if you'll excuse me . . .''

He nodded stiffly to Gaunt, and walked away. The sorcerer watched him go, his face carefully impassive. Something was wrong; he could feel it. Stalker might talk calmly enough, but the man was definitely on edge. Still, it wasn't likely he'd make any trouble. Not here, not at William's party. Gaunt frowned. Just the same, perhaps he'd better have a word with Bowman; see if he knew anything. If something had happened to upset Stalker, he'd make a dangerous enemy.

Lord and Lady Hightower stood together, a little apart from the rest of the guests. Lord Roderik looked out over the gathering, his eyes vague and far away. Lady Elaine put a gentle hand on his arm.

"You look pale, my dear. Are you feeling all right?"

"I'm fine. Really."

"You don't look it."

"It's the heat, that's all. I hate being trapped in the city during the summer. Damn place is like an oven, and there's never a breath of fresh air. I'll be all right, Elaine. Don't fuss."

Lady Elaine hesitated. "I saw you talking to the Guards. That is him, isn't it?"

"Yes. He let our boy die."

"No, Rod. It wasn't that man Hawk's fault, and you know it. You can't go on blaming him for what happened. Do you blame yourself for every soldier under your command who died in battle because you didn't predict everything that could go wrong? Of course you don't."

"This wasn't a soldier. This was our son."

"Yes, Rod. I know."

"I was so proud of him, Elaine. He wasn't going to waste his life fighting other people's battles; he was going to make something of his life. I was so proud of him. . . ."

"I miss him as much as you, my dear. But he's gone now, and we have to get on with our lives. And you've more important things to do than waste your time feuding with a Captain of the city Guard.''

Lord Roderik sighed, and looked at her properly for the first time. For a moment it seemed he was going to say something, and then he changed his mind. He looked down at her hand on his arm, and put his hand on top of hers. ''You're right, my dear. As usual. Just keep that man out of my sight. I don't want to have to talk to Captain Hawk again.''

Stalker picked up one of the canapés and studied it dubiously. The small piece of meat rolled in pasta looked even smaller in his huge hand. He sniffed at it gingerly, shrugged, and ate it anyway. When you're out in the wilds for days on end you can't ever be sure where your next meal's coming from. So you eat what you can, when you can, or risk going hungry. Old habits die hard. Stalker looked about him, and his gaze fell on Graham Dorimant, talking with the witch Visage. Stalker's lip curled. Dorimant. Political adviser. Probably never drew a sword in anger in his life. All mouth and no muscle. He had his uses, but . . . Stalker shook his head resignedly. These were the kinds of people he was going to have to deal with, now that he'd entered the political arena. Stalker smiled suddenly. He'd thought life in the wilds was tough, until he'd entered politics. These people would eat you alive, given half a chance.

And politics was going to have to be his life, from now on. He was getting too old for heroics. He didn't feel old, but he had to face the fact that he just wasn't as strong or as fast as he once was. Better to quit now, while he was still ahead. He hadn't lasted this long by being stupid. Besides, politics had its own rewards and excitements. The pursuit of power . . . Long ago, when he was young and foolish, a princess of a far-off land had offered to marry

him, and make him king, but he'd turned her down. He
hadn't wanted to be tied down. Things were different now.
He had money, and he had prestige, so what was there left
to reach for, except power? The last great game, the last
challenge. Stalker frowned suddenly. Everything had been
going fine. He and William had been an unbeatable team,
until . . . Damn the man. If only he hadn't proved so
stubborn. . . . Still, there wouldn't be any more argu-
ments after tonight. After tonight, he'd be free to go his
own way, and to hell with William Blackstone.

Stalker looked over at the young witch Visage, and
smiled slightly. Not bad-looking. Not bad at all. Not quite
to his usual taste, but there was a quiet innocence in her
demure mouth and downcast eyes that appealed to him.
It's your lucky night, my girl. He moved over to join her
and Dorimant. They both bowed politely to him, but
Stalker didn't miss the barely suppressed anger in Dorimant's eyes.

"Good evening, sir warrior," said Dorimant smoothly.
"You honour us with your presence."

"Good to see you again," said Stalker. "Keeping busy,
are you? Still digging up secrets and hauling skeletons out
of cupboards?"

"We all do what we're best at," said Dorimant.

"And how are you, my dear?" said Stalker to Visage.
"You're looking very lovely."

"Thank you," said Visage quietly. She glanced at him
briefly and then lowered her eyes again.

"Not drinking?" said Stalker, seeing her hands were
empty. "Let me get you some wine."

"Thank you, no," said Visage quickly. "I don't care
for wine. It interferes with my concentration."

"But that's why we drink it, my child," said Stalker,

grinning. "Still, the alcohol in wine needn't always be a problem. Watch this."

He poured himself a large glass of white wine from a handy decanter, and then held up the glass before him. He said half a dozen words in a quick, rasping whisper, and the wine stirred briefly in the glass, as though disturbed by an unseen presence. It quickly settled itself, and the wine looked no different than it had before.

"Try it now," said Stalker, handing the glass to Visage. "All the taste of wine, but no alcohol."

Visage sipped the wine tentatively.

"Good trick," said Hawk.

Stalker looked quickly round. He hadn't heard the Guard approach. *Getting old,* he thought sourly. *And careless.* He bowed politely to Hawk.

"A simple transformation spell," he said calmly. "The wine doesn't change its basic nature, of course; that would be beyond my simple abilities. The alcohol is still there; it just can't affect you anymore. It's a handy trick to know, on occasion. There are times when a man's survival can rest on his ability to keep a clear head."

"I can imagine," said Hawk. "But I always thought you distrusted magic, sir warrior. That seems to be the one thing all the songs about you agree on."

"Oh, them." Stalker shrugged dismissively. "I never wrote any of them. When you get right down to it, magic's a tool, like any other; just a little more complicated than most. It's not that I distrust magic; I just don't trust those who rely on it too much. Sorcery isn't like a sword or a pike; magic can let you down. And besides, I don't trust the deals some people make to gain their knowledge and power."

He looked at Gaunt on the far side of the room, and his

eyes were very cold. Hawk looked thoughtfully at Stalker. Dorimant and Visage looked at each other.

"Thank you for the wine, sir warrior," said Visage. "It's really very nice. But now, if you'll excuse us, Graham and I need to discuss some business with the Hightowers."

"And I must return to my partner," said Hawk.

They bowed politely, and then moved quickly away, leaving Stalker standing alone, staring after Visage. *You rotten little bitch,* he thought finally. *Ah, well, she wasn't really my type anyway.*

The sorcerer Gaunt raised his voice above the babble of conversation, and called for everyone's attention. The noise quickly died away as they all turned to face him.

"My friends, dinner will soon be ready. If you would like to go up to your rooms and change, I will be serving the first course in thirty minutes."

The guests moved unhurriedly out of the parlour and into the hall, talking cheerfully among themselves. Gaunt disappeared after them, presumably to check on how the first course was coming along. Hawk and Fisher were left alone in the great parlour.

"Change for dinner?" said Hawk.

"Of course," said Fisher. "We're among the Quality now."

"Makes a change," said Hawk dryly, and they both laughed.

"I'm getting rid of this cloak," said Fisher. "I don't care if we are representing the Guard; it's too damned hot to wear a cloak."

She took it off and draped it carelessly over the nearest chair. Hawk grinned, and did the same. They looked wistfully at the great table at the rear of the parlour, covered with a pristine white tablecloth and gleaming plates and cutlery. There was even a massive candelabrum in the middle of the table, with all the candles already lit.

"That looks nice," said Hawk.

"Very nice," said Fisher. "I wonder if we're invited to dinner."

"I doubt it," said Hawk. "We probably get scraps and leftovers in the kitchen, afterwards. Unless Blackstone decides he wants a food taster, and I think Gaunt would probably take that as an insult to his culinary arts."

"Ah, well," said Fisher. "At least now we can sit down for a while. My feet are killing me."

"Right," said Hawk. "It's been a long day. . . ."

They drew up chairs by the empty fireplace, dropped into them, and stretched out their legs. The chairs were almost indecently comfortable and supportive. Hawk and Fisher sat in silence a while, almost dozing. The unrelenting muggy heat weighed down on them, making sleep seem very tempting. The minutes passed pleasantly and Hawk stretched lazily. And then Katherine Blackstone came hurrying into the parlour, and Hawk sat up with a jolt as he saw the worry in her face.

"I'm sorry to trouble you," said Katherine hesitantly.

"Not at all," said Hawk. "That's what we're here for."

"It's my husband," said Katherine. "He went into our room to get changed while I paid a visit to the bathroom. When I came back, the door to our room was locked from the inside. I knocked and called, but there was no answer. I'm afraid he may have been taken ill or something."

Hawk and Fisher looked quickly at each other, and got to their feet.

"I think we'd better take a look," said Hawk. "Just in case. If you'd show us the way, please . . ."

Katherine Blackstone nodded quickly, and led them out of the parlour and into the hall. Hawk's hand rested on the

axe at his side. He had a bad feeling about this. Katherine
hurried down the hall and up the stairs at the far end,
grabbing at the banister as though to pull herself along
faster. Hawk and Fisher had to push themselves to keep
up with her. Katherine reached the top of the stairs first,
and ran down the landing to the third door on the left. She
hammered on the door and rattled the doorknob, then
looked worriedly at Hawk.

"It's still locked, Captain. William! William, can you
hear me?" There was no reply. Katherine stepped back
and looked desperately at Hawk. "Use your axe. Smash
the lock. I'll take the responsibility."

Hawk frowned as he drew his axe. "Perhaps we should
talk to Gaunt first. . . ."

"I'm not waiting! William could be ill in there. Break
the door down now. That's an order, Captain!"

Hawk nodded, and took a good grip on his axe. "Stand
back, then, and give me some room."

"What the hell is going on here?" said Gaunt, from the
top of the stairs. "Captain, put down your axe."

Hawk looked steadily at the sorcerer. "Councillor
Blackstone doesn't answer our calls, and his door is locked
from the inside. Do you have a spare key?"

Gaunt came forward to join him. "No," he said slowly,
"I've never needed any spares." He looked at the closed
door, and his mouth tightened. "William could be hurt.
Smash the lock."

Hawk nodded, and swung his axe at the brass lock,
using all his strength. The blade sank deep into the wood,
and the keen edge bit into the brass. The heavy door shook
violently in its frame, but didn't open. Hawk jerked the
blade free, and struck again. The axe sheared clean
through the lock. Hawk smiled slightly as he pulled the
blade free. It was a good axe. He kicked the door open,

and he and Fisher hurried into the room, with Katherine and Gaunt close behind.

William Blackstone lay on his back on the floor, staring sightlessly at the ceiling. A knife hilt protruded from his chest, and his shirtfront was red with blood.

3

Questions and Answers

Katherine Blackstone pushed past Hawk and Fisher, and ran forward to kneel beside her husband. Her hand went briefly to his chest, and then to his face. She looked back at Hawk, and her face was blank and confused.

"He's dead. He's really dead. Who . . . Who . . ."

She suddenly started to cry, great rasping sobs that shook her whole body. Fisher moved forward and knelt beside her for a moment before putting an arm round her shoulders and helping her to her feet. She led Katherine away from the body and made her sit down on the bed. Katherine accepted this docilely. Tears rolled down her face, but she made no attempt to wipe them away. Shock. Hawk had seen it before. He looked at Gaunt, standing beside him in the doorway. The sorcerer looked shaken and confused, unable to take in what had happened.

"Gaunt," said Hawk quietly, "You're her friend; get her out of here. Fisher and I have to examine the body."

"Of course," said Gaunt. "I'm sorry, I . . . of course."

"And, Gaunt . . ."

"Yes?"

"Take her downstairs, get somebody to sit with her, and then set up an isolation spell. I don't want anyone or anything getting in or out of this house."

"Yes. I understand."

Gaunt went over to Katherine and spoke softly to her. Katherine shook her head dazedly, but got to her feet as Gaunt went on talking to her, his voice low and calm and persuasive. They left the room together, and Hawk shut the door behind them. Hawk and Fisher looked at the dead body, and then at each other.

"Some bodyguards we turned out to be," said Hawk.

Fisher nodded disgustedly. "This is going to be a real mess, Hawk. Blackstone was the best thing to happen to this city in years. What's going to happen with him gone?"

"If we don't find out who killed him, and quickly, there'll be riots in the streets," said Hawk grimly. "Damn. I liked him, Isobel. He trusted us to keep him safe, and we let him down."

"Come on," said Fisher. "We've got work to do. I'll check the room, you check the body."

Hawk nodded, and knelt down beside Blackstone. He looked the body over from head to toe, careful not to touch anything. Blackstone's face was calm and relaxed, the eyes open and staring at the ceiling. His hands were empty. One leg had buckled under him as he fell back, and was trapped beneath the other. The knife had been driven into his heart with such strength that the crosspiece of the knife was flush with Blackstone's chest. Hawk looked at the weapon closely, but it seemed a perfectly ordinary knife. There were no other wounds on the body, or any sign that Blackstone had tried to defend himself. The shirt around the knife was soaked with blood. Hawk frowned. With a wound like that, you'd expect a lot more blood. . . .

"Look at this," said Fisher.

Hawk looked up sharply.

Fisher was crouched down beside the bed, staring at a wineglass lying on its side on the thick rug. There was a little red wine left in the glass, and a few drops had spilled out onto the rug. The crimson stains looked disturbingly like blood. Fisher dipped a finger into the wine in the glass, and then lifted it to her mouth.

"Don't," said Hawk. "It could be poisoned."

Fisher sniffed at her finger. "Smells okay."

"Leave it anyway, until we've had a chance to check it."

"Come on, Hawk. Why poison Blackstone and then stab him through the heart?"

"All right, I'll admit it's highly unlikely. But you never know. Wipe your fingers off thoroughly, okay?"

"Okay." Fisher wiped her finger on the bedspread, and then moved over to crouch down beside Hawk. She stared glumly at the body, and shook her head slowly. "Well. How do you see it happening?"

Hawk frowned. "The door was locked from the inside, and Blackstone had the only key. At least, I assume he had it. I'll check in a minute to make sure. Anyway, I think we're fairly safe in assuming it wasn't suicide. First, he had everything to live for. Second, there had been threats on his life. And third, he'd have a hell of a hard job stabbing himself like that. Apart from anything else, the angle's all wrong. No, suicide is definitely out."

"Right," said Fisher. "So, somebody got in here, stabbed Blackstone, and then left, leaving the door locked from the inside. Tricky. Could Blackstone have locked the door himself, after he was stabbed?"

"No," said Hawk. "With a wound like that, he must have died instantly."

"Yeah," said Fisher. "All right. Who could have killed Blackstone? It had to be one of the guests. A stranger would have one hell of a hard time getting into Gaunt's house, and even if he had, Blackstone would have taken one look at him and yelled the place down. And since he was stabbed in the chest, he must have seen his attacker."

"Right," said Hawk. "So, if Blackstone saw whoever it was, and didn't cry out, that can only mean he knew his attacker, and didn't consider him a threat until it was too late."

"Nasty," said Fisher.

"Very," said Hawk. "I'd better make sure Gaunt's set up the isolation spell. I don't want any of our guests disappearing before I have a chance to question them. You stay with the body. No one is to touch anything, right?"

"Right."

Hawk straightened up and stretched slowly. "You know, Isobel, this is going to be a complicated case. I can feel it in my bones."

He left Blackstone's room and went out onto the landing, pulling the door shut behind him. The guests were crowded together on the landing, waiting for him. Lord Hightower stepped forward to block Hawk's way.

"You. Guard! What's going on?"

"My Lord . . ."

"Why have you smashed down William's door?" demanded Bowman. "Gaunt took Katherine away in tears, but he wouldn't tell us anything. Just said we weren't to go in the room. What's happened?"

"William Blackstone has been murdered," said Hawk tightly.

The guests stared silently back at him, all of them apparently shocked and stunned.

"I have instructed the sorcerer Gaunt to seal off the

house," said Hawk. "Have any of you seen or heard anything suspicious? Anything at all?" There was a general shaking of heads, which was pretty much what Hawk had expected. He sighed quietly. "I have to talk to the sorcerer. My partner is guarding the body. I must ask you all not to enter Councillor Blackstone's room for any reason, until the investigation into his death is over. I suggest you all go downstairs and wait in the parlour, and I'll fill you in on the details of what's happened as soon as I can."

He turned quickly away before they could start asking questions, and hurried down the stairs to find Gaunt.

Fisher moved slowly around Blackstone's room, looking for anything out of the ordinary. She'd tried all the obvious things, like looking in the wardrobe and under the bed, but so far the only clue to be found was the wineglass. Fisher scowled. The trouble with searching for clues was that half the time you didn't know what you were looking for until you found it. And even then, you couldn't be sure. She stood still in the middle of the room and looked about her. The color scheme was a little garish for her taste, but there was no denying that all the furniture and fittings were of the best possible quality. Nothing seemed to have been moved, or in any way disturbed. Everything was as it should be. Fisher glanced down at Blackstone's body, and scowled thoughtfully. The killer had to be one of the guests, but they were all supposed to be friends of the dead man. One of them must have a motive. Find the motive, and you find the killer. . . . Fisher sat down on the edge of the bed and methodically worked her way through the list of suspects again.

Katherine Blackstone had looked to be very fond of Edward Bowman. Perhaps she'd grown tired of being married to a man ten years older than herself, and had decided

to get rid of him so that she could take up with a younger
man.

Lord Hightower claimed to have joined with Blackstone
because of the way he'd been treated by the city Council,
but that could have been just a cover, a way of getting
close to Blackstone. And Lord Roderik was a military
man; he'd know how to kill quickly and silently. But then
again, why should he want to? Blackstone just wasn't that
important, outside of Haven.

And then there was the death wound itself. It must have
taken quite a bit of strength to ram the knife all the way
home. A great deal of strength . . . or desperation.

Fisher shook her head. There was no point in making
guesses at this stage. She didn't have enough evidence to
go on yet. The door creaked loudly as it swung suddenly
open, and Fisher leapt to her feet, sword in hand, as Lord
Hightower entered the room.

"That's far enough, my Lord."

Hightower glared at her coldly. "Watch your manners,
girl. I'm here to take a look at the body."

"I'm afraid I can't allow that, my Lord."

"You'll do as you're damn well told. I still have my
rank as General. . . ."

"And that doesn't count a damn with me," said Fisher
politely. "As the only Guards present, Hawk and I have
taken charge of the investigation. And at the scene of the
crime, we are answerable only to our superior officers.
That's city law, Lord Hightower. Now I'm afraid I must
insist that you leave. I can't risk you accidentally destroy-
ing any evidence."

Hightower started forward, and then stopped dead as
Fisher raised her sword. He took in her calm, professional
stance, and the old scars that scored her muscular forearm.
The sword point didn't waver, and neither did her nar-

rowed eyes. Hightower stared at her coldly, and stepped back a pace.

"You'll regret this, Guard," he said softly. "I'll see to that."

He turned and left, slamming the door shut behind him. Fisher lowered her sword. Some days you just shouldn't get out of bed.

Downstairs, Hawk stood in the middle of the hall and looked around him, but there was no sign of Gaunt. Katherine Blackstone was sitting alone in the parlour. She had a glass of wine in her hand, but she wasn't drinking it. She just sat in a chair by the empty fireplace, staring at nothing. A door opened behind Hawk and he spun round, axe in hand, to see Gaunt stepping into the hall from the room opposite the parlour.

"Where the hell have you been?" said Hawk quietly, not wanting to disturb Katherine.

"Just checking my defences," said Gaunt. "I can assure you that apart from those I invited, no one has got in or out of this house, before or since the murder. I'm now ready to set up the isolation spell. Are you sure you want to do this, Captain? Once the spell is established, this house and everyone in it will be sealed off from the outside world until dawn. That's a good seven hours."

"Do it," said Hawk. "I know; these are important people, and they're not going to like being held here against their will, but I can't risk letting the killer escape. In the meantime, I really don't think we should leave Katherine on her own. I thought I told you to find someone to sit with her?"

"There wasn't time," said Gaunt. "I thought it was more important to check my defences, in case the assassin was still here. Believe me, Katherine will be perfectly all right on her own for a few minutes. I've given her a specific of my own devising; it should help to stave off the shock.''

Hawk frowned. ''It won't knock her out, will it? I'm going to have to ask her some questions in a while.''

''No, it's only a mild sedative. Now, if you've finished with me for the moment, I think I'd better set up the isolation spell.'' The sorcerer's mouth twisted angrily. ''I still can't really believe that one of my guests murdered William . . . but I suppose I must.''

Gaunt strode down the hall to stand before the closed front door. He stood motionless for a long moment, and then said a single word aloud. The sound of it echoed loudly on the air, and Hawk clutched tightly at the shaft of his axe as Gaunt's hands began to glow with an eerie blue light. The atmosphere in the hall grew tense and brittle, and Hawk could feel a pressure building on the air. Gaunt threw up his arms in the stance of summoning, and his hands glowed so brightly it hurt to look at them. His mouth moved soundlessly, his eyes squeezed shut as he concentrated. Hawk winced as a juddering vibration ran suddenly through his bones, chattering his teeth. And then the sorcerer spoke a single Word of Power, and a deafening roar filled the whole house. Hawk staggered as the floor shook beneath his feet and then grew still. The sound was suddenly gone. Hawk got his balance back and looked around him. Everything seemed to be normal again. The sorcerer walked back to join him. Hawk glanced quickly at Gaunt's hands, but they were no longer glowing.

''The spell is set,'' said Gaunt. ''It cannot be broken. So if there is a murderer in my house, we're trapped in here with him until first light. I do hope you know what you're doing, Captain Hawk.''

''There is a murderer,'' said Hawk calmly, ''and I'll

get him. Now let's go back upstairs. I want you to take another look at Blackstone's body.''

Gaunt nodded briefly, and Hawk sheathed his axe and led the way back down the hall to the stairs. The guests had all assembled in the parlour, but Hawk didn't stop to talk to them. They could wait a while. He and Gaunt made their way up the stairs and onto the landing. Gaunt stopped before the door to Blackstone's room and looked hard at Hawk. He took in the scarred wood and shattered lock, and shrugged. Gaunt sighed audibly, and looked away. Hawk pushed open the door and walked in, followed by Gaunt.

Fisher looked up sharply, and then put away her sword as she saw who it was. Hawk raised an eyebrow.

"Any problems while I was gone?"

"Not really," said Fisher, "I had to throw Lord Hightower out. He wanted to examine the body.''

"You threw him out?" said Gaunt.

"Of course," said Hawk. "We're in charge at the scene of a crime. Always. That's Haven law. On such occasions, anyone refusing to obey a Guard's lawful orders, or failing to answer his questions, is liable to a heavy fine or a stay in prison.''

"That sounded suspiciously like a threat," said Gaunt.

"Just trying to clarify the situation, sir sorcerer," said Hawk.

Gaunt nodded stiffly. "Of course. I'm sorry, I'm a little over-sensitive at the moment; I'm rather upset. I suppose we all are. William's death is a great loss to us all.''

"Not to everyone, it isn't," said Fisher. "Somebody must have stood to gain by it. All we have to do is work out why, and then we should have our murderer. That's the theory, anyway.''

"I see," said Gaunt.

Hawk frowned slightly. He'd been watching the sorcerer closely, and Gaunt's perpetual calmness was beginning to get on his nerves. The sorcerer might claim to be upset over his friend's death, but if he was, he was doing a damn good job of hiding it. In fact, if William had been the close friend that Gaunt claimed him to be, the sorcerer was being suspiciously cool and collected. Then again, sorcerers weren't exactly famous for behaving normally. If they were normal, they wouldn't have become sorcerers in the first place.

"Well," said Gaunt, "I'm here. What do you want of me, Captain Hawk?"

"I'm not really sure," said Hawk. "I don't know that much about sorcery. Is there anything your magic can do to help us detect or re-create the events leading up to William's murder?"

Gaunt frowned slightly. "I'm afraid not. My magic isn't really suited to such work. You see, all sorcerers specialise in their own particular area of interest. Some deal with transformational magic, others with weather control, constructs and homunculi, spirits of the air and of the deep. . . . We all start out with the same basic grounding in the four elements, but after that . . . the High Magic takes many forms."

"What is your specialisation?" asked Fisher patiently.

"Alchemy," said Gaunt. "Medicines, and the like."

"And poisons?" said Hawk.

"On occasion." Gaunt looked at Hawk sharply. "Did you have any reason for such a question?"

"Possibly." Hawk indicated the wineglass lying on the rug beside the bed. "It seems likely Blackstone was drinking from that glass just before he was attacked. Can you tell whether or not the wine had been poisoned?"

"I'll need a sample to test before I can be sure," said

Gaunt. "But I can tell you straightaway whether the wine contained anything harmful. That's a simple spell."

He stretched out his left hand towards the wineglass and muttered something under his breath. A cold breeze seemed to blow suddenly through the room, and then was gone. Gaunt shook his head, and lowered his arm. "It's perfectly harmless." He knelt down beside the glass, dipped his finger into the remaining dregs, and then sucked his finger clean. "One of my better wines. I'll run some checks in my laboratory, just to be sure there isn't anything else in it, like a mild soporific, but I'm sure my spell would have detected even that. May I take the glass?"

"I'm afraid not," said Hawk. "That has to stay where it is for the moment. We may need it for evidence later on. But you're welcome to take a sample of the wine itself; just don't disturb the glass."

Gaunt hesitated. "Captain Hawk, there's something else . . . something unusual in this room."

"Where?" said Hawk quickly.

"I don't know, but it's definitely something magical." Gaunt frowned, and looked at Blackstone's body. "Perhaps William was carrying a protective charm of some kind."

Hawk looked at Fisher. "Have you searched the body?"

"Not yet. I was waiting for you to get back."

"All right; let's take a look."

Hawk knelt down beside Blackstone's body, took a deep breath to steady himself, and started with the jerkin pockets. He found two handkerchiefs, one badly in need of a wash, and a handful of loose change. He dumped both the handkerchiefs and the money beside the body, then tried the trouser pockets. Some more loose change, and a half dozen visiting cards. Hawk dumped them with his other finds. He thought a moment, and then carefully undid

Blackstone's high collar. He nodded slowly as the stiff cloth fell away to reveal a silver chain around the dead man's neck. Using only his fingertips, Hawk pulled gently at the chain until the amulet it held came out from under the dead man's shirt. It was a bone amulet, with a series of tiny runes etched deep into the bone. It was spotted with the dead man's blood. Hawk held it up so that Gaunt could see it.

"Do you know what this is, sir sorcerer?"

"Yes. It's an amulet of protection. The witch Visage made it for William. I tested it for her myself a few days ago, to make sure it would work. It was designed to protect the wearer against magical attacks. Any spell aimed at William would have ceased to work in his vicinity. A very useful defence."

"So curses and the like would have had no effect on him?" said Fisher slowly.

"Not as long as he wore the amulet," said Gaunt. "Anything of a magical nature would cease to be magical once it came anywhere near William. It would become magical again once it had moved beyond the amulet's sphere of influence, of course."

"Of course," said Hawk. He dropped the amulet onto Blackstone's chest. "How big a sphere of influence would such an amulet have?"

"No more than a few inches. It's not a very powerful amulet, but then, it doesn't need to be."

"So whatever else happens," said Fisher, "we can safely assume that Councillor Blackstone wasn't killed by magic?"

"I don't see how he could have been," said Gaunt.

"Thank you, sir sorcerer," said Hawk. "You've been very helpful. Perhaps you would now be so kind as to join your guests in the parlour. My partner and I will join you shortly."

"Very well," said Gaunt. He looked from Hawk to Fisher, and then settled on Hawk, his dark eyes steady and disconcertingly cold. "William was my friend. I don't think I've ever known a man I admired more. I'll do everything I can to help you find the man who killed him. I give you my word on it."

He nodded abruptly to them both, turned quickly on his heel, and left. Hawk sat down on the bed and stared moodily at the dead man. Fisher leaned lazily against the wall.

"A very pretty exit speech," she said calmly.

"Very," said Hawk. "I hope he doesn't turn out to be the murderer. Trying to arrest a sorcerer as powerful as he's supposed to be might prove rather difficult. Not to mention extremely dangerous. On the other hand, if he isn't our killer, we'd better find the man responsible before Gaunt does. At least with us he'd live to stand trial."

"Yeah." Fisher leaned her head back against the wall and frowned thoughtfully at the ceiling. "Do we assume that Gaunt is right, and Blackstone wasn't killed by magic?"

"It's a simple choice," said Hawk. "Either the amulet is what Gaunt said it is, or it isn't. If it is, Blackstone couldn't have been killed by magic. But if Gaunt was lying . . ."

"Unlikely. He must have known we'd check with Visage."

"Unless they're working together."

"I hate conspiracies," said Fisher.

"Yeah," said Hawk. "And I hate it when there's magic involved; it complicates the hell out of a case."

"Have you found the key yet?" said Fisher suddenly, looking vaguely about her.

"Damn. Knew I forgot something." Hawk scowled down at the dead man. "It wasn't in his pockets." He got to his feet and looked around him.

He and Fisher moved back and forth around the room, but couldn't see anything that even looked like a key. Finally they both got down on their hands and knees and started combing through the thick rugs with their fingers.

"Here!" said Fisher. She clambered awkwardly to her feet, holding up a key she'd found by the door. "It must have been left in the keyhole, and fell out when you smashed the lock."

"Assuming that is the right key," said Hawk, getting to his feet.

"Oh, come on, Hawk! What are the odds on there happening to be another key lying on the floor right by the door?"

Hawk smiled and shrugged. "Sorry, lass. That's the trouble with cases like this; you start doubting everything. We'll show Gaunt the key, and he can tell us for sure."

"Why don't we just try it in the lock?"

"Because after what I did to that lock with my axe, no key would work it."

Fisher glanced at the smashed lock, and nodded reluctantly. "I see what you mean. We'll ask Gaunt." She slipped the key into her trouser pocket.

"All right," said Hawk, "let's try and re-create what happened here. Blackstone was stabbed with a knife. The door was locked from the inside. So how did the killer get in and out?"

"Teleport?" said Fisher.

Hawk frowned. "It's possible, I suppose, but a spell like that takes a lot of power and a hell of a lot of expertise. And the only person here who fits that description is . . ."

"Gaunt," said Fisher.

"Visage wouldn't have the power," said Hawk. "Would she?"

"So far, this case has been nothing but questions with no trustworthy answers," said Fisher disgustedly. "This case is going to be a challenge. I hate challenges. We were better off with the vampire. At least we knew where we were with him."

"Come on," said Hawk. "Let's go down and face the crowd in the parlour. Maybe we can get some answers out of them."

"We might," said Fisher. "But I doubt it."

They left the room, and Hawk pulled the door shut behind him. It wouldn't stay closed. Hawk looked at the splintered wood and the shattered lock, and wasn't surprised.

"You always were efficient," said Fisher, smiling. "But if we can't lock the door, how are we going to keep people out?"

"Beats me," said Hawk. "Ask them nicely? There's not a lot in the room in the way of real evidence, as far as I can tell. . . . And any attempt to interfere with the scene of the crime would be a pretty good indication of guilt. So let's just leave the door open and see what happens."

"I love it when you're devious," said Fisher.

They chuckled quietly together, and made their way down the stairs and into the parlour. Hawk and Fisher paused a moment in the doorway, taking in the waiting suspects. The sorcerer Gaunt stood at the rear of the room by the main table. His face was calm, but his eyes were dark and brooding. Katherine Blackstone was still sitting in her chair by the empty fireplace. Her eyes were red and puffy from crying, and she had a tired, defeated look. Bowman stood beside her. His face was calm and controlled, as always. The Lord and Lady Hightower stood together by the buffet table. Their backs were straight and their heads erect, and they stood protectively close to each other. Hawk looked at the Lady Elaine's hands. They were held tightly together, the knuckles white from the pressure, as though to stop them trembling. Anger? Or fear? Not far away, Dorimant was helping himself to another glass of the fruit cordial. His normally ruddy face was pale and strained, and his hands were unsteady. The witch Visage stood beside him. She looked lost and frightened and very young. As Hawk watched, Dorimant put his arm around the witch's shoulders. Visage leaned against him gratefully, as though all the strength had gone out of her. Adam Stalker stood alone in the middle of the room. He glared impatiently at Hawk and Fisher as they stood in the doorway.

"Well?" he said finally. "What's happened? And why have we been kept waiting all this time?"

"Councillor Blackstone is dead," said Hawk quietly. He waited a moment, but no one said anything. Hawk walked forward into the parlour with Fisher at his side, and Stalker reluctantly gave way to allow them to take up the centre position. Hawk looked slowly about him, to be sure he had everyone's attention, and then continued. "William Blackstone was stabbed to death, in his room. So far, we have no clues as to the identity of the killer. At my request, the sorcerer Gaunt has sealed off the house with an isolation spell. No one can get in or out."

The guests stirred uneasily, but still nobody said anything. For a moment, Hawk thought Hightower might. His face had lost all its color, and his hands had clenched into fists. But the moment passed, and Hightower remained silent. Hawk took a deep breath, and continued.

"Now, as Guards, my partner and I are required to question you each in turn, to help build up a picture of what was happening at the time of the killing. In the meantime, of course, no one is to go near the body."

"Wait a minute," said Bowman. "Question us? Are you saying you think one of us is the killer?"

"Ridiculous!" snapped Hightower. "And I'm damned if I'm answering any questions from a jumped-up Guard!"

"Refusal to assist us in our enquiries is in itself a crime," said Fisher calmly. "I'm sure you all know the penalties for obstructing the Guard in the performance of their duty."

"You wouldn't dare. . . ." said Hightower.

"Wouldn't I?" said Hawk. He locked eyes with Hightower, and Hightower was the first to look away. Stalker stepped forward.

"I've had experience with murders before, Captain. If I can help in any way, you have only to ask."

"Thank you, sir Stalker," said Hawk politely. "I'll bear that in mind." He turned to Gaunt. "Sir sorcerer, is there a room my partner and I can use to talk privately with your guests?"

"Of course, Captain. There's my library; it's just across the hall."

The library proved to be a small, cosy room directly opposite the parlour. Gaunt ushered Hawk and Fisher in, and lit two of the library's oil lamps with a wave of his hand. All four of the walls were lined with bookshelves, each packed with books of various shapes and sizes. The books were stacked neatly, though apparently according to size and shape as much as contents. There were two comfortable-looking chairs by the empty fireplace, and two other doors, one to the left and one to the right.

"Where do they lead?" said Hawk, indicating the doors.

"The door to your right leads to the kitchen," said Gaunt. "The door to your left leads to my private laboratory. That door is locked and shielded at all times."

"Fine," said Hawk. "This room should do nicely. I think we'll make a start with you, sir Gaunt, if it's convenient."

"Of course," said Gaunt. "But we'll need another chair." He gestured sharply, and the library door swung open. A chair came sliding out of the parlour. It crossed the hall and entered the library, and the door swung shut behind it. Gaunt carefully positioned the chair before the empty fireplace and sat down. Hawk and Fisher pulled up the other two chairs, and sat facing him.

"That was very impressive," said Hawk.

"Not really," said Gaunt. "Well, what do we do now? I've never been involved in a murder investigation before. What kind of things do you need to ask me?"

"Nothing too difficult," said Hawk. "To start with, do you recognise this key?" He nodded to Fisher, who dug the key out of her pocket and handed it to Gaunt. The sorcerer looked at the key, and then turned it over in his hand a few times.

"It looks like one of mine. Is it the key to William's room?"

"That's what we want to know."

Gaunt shrugged. "All the keys look the same to me. Since I live on my own most of the time, I don't have much use for the upstairs rooms. Usually I keep all my keys on one ring, in the right order so that I can tell them apart. And now they've all been split up. . . . Still, it shouldn't be too difficult to work out which key it is. Where did you find it?''

"In Blackstone's room," said Fisher. "On the floor, not far from the door."

Gaunt looked at Hawk. "Then why ask me if this is William's key?"

"Because in a case like this we need to be very sure of our facts," said Hawk. "You can never tell what's going to turn out to be significant. Please let me know when you're sure that's Blackstone's key. Now, sir Gaunt, what did you do earlier this evening, after your guests had gone upstairs to change?"

"I went into the kitchen," said Gaunt. "The meal was almost ready. All I had to do was pour the soup into the bowls, and baste the meat one last time. I did that, and then I thought I'd better check that the table was ready. I walked out into the hall, and that was when I sensed the murder."

Fisher leaned forward in her chair. "You *sensed* the murder?"

"Oh, yes," said Gaunt. "I didn't know what it was at the time. I just felt a disturbance in the house, as though something terrible had happened. I ran upstairs to check that my guests were all right, and that's when I found you preparing to cut down my door with an axe. You know the rest."

"Yes," said Hawk thoughtfully. "Tell me, sir Gaunt, could anyone use a teleport spell in this house without you knowing?"

"A teleport? Certainly not. Such spells take a great deal of power and skill to bring off correctly. One small mistake in the arrival coordinates, and you'd have a very nasty accident. I can see what you're getting at, Captain Hawk, but there's no way the assassin could have teleported into

William's room and out again. I have wards set up all over the house to prevent just such a thing. I have my enemies too, you know. Even I couldn't teleport in this house, without first dismantling the wards.''

''I see,'' said Hawk. ''Perhaps we should discuss Councillor Blackstone's enemies. It's common knowledge he was unpopular in some quarters, but can you suggest any names? Especially anyone who would profit by his death.''

''There's no one in particular,'' said Gaunt, frowning. ''There are any number of people in Haven who'll breathe easier, knowing that William is dead, but I can't think of anyone insane enough to murder William in my house. They must have known that I would take this as a personal insult.''

''I see your point,'' said Hawk dryly.

''There is one thing,'' said Gaunt, and then he hesitated. Hawk waited patiently. Gaunt looked at him steadily. ''I really don't know if this is at all relevant. I feel rather foolish even mentioning it, but . . . William had an argument recently, with Adam Stalker. I don't know what it was about, but it must have been serious. They've hardly spoken to each other for weeks.''

''You did the right thing in telling us,'' said Hawk. ''I shouldn't think it means anything, but we'll check it out, just in case. I think that's all for the moment, sir Gaunt. You can rejoin the others in the parlour now. And tell the witch Visage we'd like to see her next.''

''Of course,'' said Gaunt. ''I'll send her in.'' He got to his feet and crossed to the door. It swung open before him, and then he hesitated in the doorway and looked back at Hawk. ''What should I do about dinner?''

''Serve it if you like,'' said Fisher. ''But I think you'll find most people have lost their appetite.''

Gaunt nodded, and left. The door swung shut behind him. Hawk looked at Fisher.

"How am I doing?"

"Not bad," said Fisher. "Just the right mix of authority and politeness. Do you believe him about the anti-teleport wards?"

"Makes sense to me," said Hawk. "Every sorcerer has enemies. And again, it's something we can check with Visage. If there are such wards in the house, she should be able to detect them."

"Good point. Now, what about the keys? Gaunt said there were no duplicates, but he could be lying. If he did have a duplicate, he could easily have let himself in, killed Blackstone, and left again, locking the door after him."

"No," said Hawk firmly. "I don't buy that. It's too obvious."

"So what? Look, there's already one hole in his story. He said that during the time of the murder he left the parlour with the guests and went into the kitchen. He poured out the soup and basted the meat, and then had his premonition about Blackstone's death. It doesn't add up, Hawk. Between everyone leaving the parlour and us breaking the door down, there had to have been at least fifteen to twenty minutes. I remember looking at the clock in the parlour. Now, it doesn't take that long to pour out some soup and baste a joint of meat. So what else was he doing?"

"Another good point," said Hawk. "But I still can't see Gaunt as the murderer. If he'd wanted to kill Blackstone, surely he would have found a more subtle way than to stab the man under his own roof. Remember the Hook? Two hundred and forty-seven dead, and nothing to connect any of them with Gaunt. The forensic magicians couldn't find a single shred of evidence against him, and it wasn't for want of trying. I think he injured their pride.''

"All right, I see what you mean.'' Fisher stirred uneasily in her chair. "But it could just be misdirection, so that we wouldn't suspect him. Remember how Gaunt used his magic to move that chair without touching it? Perhaps he could use a knife the same way. Or open a lock, just as he opened and shut that door, just by looking at it. If by some chance we find proof that Gaunt is the murderer, we'd better watch ourselves. If we start getting too close to the truth, he might decide to do something subtle about us.''

"Great,'' said Hawk. "Just great. This case is getting more fun by the minute.''

There was a hesitant knock at the door, and then the witch Visage came in. She shut the door quietly behind her and looked uncertainly from Hawk to Fisher. Hawk nodded at the empty chair, and Visage sank into it. Her face was still deathly pale, and she kept her eyes modestly downcast. Fisher looked at Hawk, who nodded slightly.

"We need to ask you some questions,'' said Fisher.

"Yes,'' said Visage. Her voice was little more than a whisper.

"Where were you when Blackstone was killed?'' said Fisher bluntly.

"In my room, I suppose. I don't know exactly when William died.''

"Gaunt said he sensed the killing,'' said Hawk. "Are you saying you didn't feel anything?''

"Yes,'' said Visage. She raised her head and met his gaze for the first time. "Gaunt is much more powerful than I'll ever be. He's a sorcerer.''

"All right, so you were in your room,'' said Fisher. "Did anyone see you there?''

"No. I was alone."

"So you can't prove you were in your room."

"No."

"Earlier this evening you said you knew why Katherine Blackstone was acting strangely," said Hawk. "But you didn't get around to telling us then. Tell us now."

"Why don't you ask Bowman?" said Visage.

Hawk and Fisher glanced quickly at each other.

"Why Bowman?" said Hawk.

Visage smiled slightly. Her green eyes were very cold. "You must have seen him and Katherine together. They're not exactly subtle about it."

"They do seem very friendly," said Fisher.

"They've been lovers for at least six months," said Visage flatly. "That's why she's always laughing and smiling. She's found another fool."

"Did Blackstone know?" asked Hawk.

"I don't think so. William could be very good at not seeing things he didn't want to."

Hawk frowned thoughtfully. "How long have you been working for Blackstone?"

"Four, five years. Since his first campaign in the Heights area. I protected him from magical threats. He's always had enemies. Good men always do."

"You gave him the amulet he wore?"

"Yes. As long as he wore it, no magic could harm him."

"You mentioned enemies," said Fisher. "Can you give us any names?"

Visage shook her head firmly. "William wasn't killed by an assassin. The only people in this house are Gaunt, his guests, and you. There is no one else. I'd have known."

"Are you sure?" said Hawk.

"Yes. At least . . ." Visage frowned slightly. "There is a part of this house that is closed to me. I can't see into it."

"Where?" said Fisher, leaning forward.

Visage looked at the left-hand door. "Gaunt's laboratory. It's surrounded by a very powerful shield. He's always been very jealous of his secrets."

"Could someone be hiding in there?" asked Hawk.

Visage shook her head. "No one could have left that room without my knowing about it."

"Then why mention the room?" said Fisher.

"Because it disturbs me," said Visage.

For a while no one said anything. Visage's words seemed to hang on the air. Hawk cleared his throat.

"Gaunt said this house was warded against teleport spells. Is that true?"

Visage nodded soberly. "Of course. It was one of the first things I checked for when I entered the house. It's not unusual; all sorcerers have such protections. Why are you wasting time with all these questions? Edward Bowman killed William. Isn't it obvious? Bowman wanted Katherine, and they both knew William would never agree to a divorce. It would have destroyed his political career."

"That's an interesting theory," said Hawk, "but we can't arrest a man without some kind of proof. For the time being, everyone is equally suspect."

"Including me?"

"Yes."

"I could never have harmed William," said Visage flatly.

Hawk studied her thoughtfully. "Earlier on, I saw Gaunt bring a chair into this room by magic. He just looked at it, and it moved. Could he have manipulated a knife in the same way?"

"Through a locked door, you mean?" Visage shook her head. "That kind of magic is simple enough, but it needs eye contact with the object to be moved."

"All right," said Hawk, "could he have used that magic to pick the lock?"

"No. There are wards in this house to prevent such tamperings."

"Of course," said Hawk. "There would be. Damn."

"I think that's all, for the moment," said Fisher. "Please wait in the parlour, and ask Bowman to come in next."

Visage sat where she was, and looked hotly at Hawk and Fisher. "You're not going to do anything, are you? Bowman's too important. He has influence. I'm warning you; I won't let him get away with this. I'll kill him first!"

She jumped to her feet and hurried out of the library, slamming the door behind her. Fisher raised an eyebrow.

"If she's prepared to kill one man, she might have killed another."

"Right," said Hawk. "There's a fire burning under that cool and quiet surface. She was obviously very fond of Blackstone. . . . Maybe she was having an affair with him. It went sour—perhaps she wanted him to divorce his wife and marry her and he refused—so she killed him for revenge. Or maybe she wanted an affair and he didn't, so she killed him out of injured pride."

"That's reaching a bit, isn't it?" said Fisher.

Hawk shrugged. "This early in the game, how can we tell?"

"No," said Fisher. "It still doesn't feel right. If there were hard feelings between Blackstone and Visage, he'd hardly have kept her on as his bodyguard, would he? I mean, that's what her job amounted to. And anyway, Visage is a witch; if she wanted to kill someone, she wouldn't need a knife to do it. . . . Unless she was trying to be misleading. . . .''

''I think we've had this conversation before,'' said Hawk dryly.

The door opened, and Bowman came in. He smiled briefly, and sat down in the empty chair without waiting to be asked. Hawk frowned slightly. For a man whose friend and employer had just been murdered, Bowman looked very composed. But then, he always did.

''You were Blackstone's right-hand man,'' said Fisher.

''That's right,'' said Bowman pleasantly.

''Would you mind telling us where you were at the time of the murder?''

''I was in my room. Changing for dinner.''

''Can anyone verify that?'' asked Hawk. Bowman looked at him steadily.

''No.''

''So you don't really have an alibi?''

Bowman smiled. ''Do I need one?''

''How long have you known William Blackstone?'' asked Fisher.

''Seven, eight years.''

''How long have you known Katherine Blackstone?'' asked Hawk.

''About the same,'' said Bowman.

Hawk and Fisher looked at him silently, but his pleasant smile didn't waver. The silence dragged on.

''Who do you think killed Blackstone?'' said Hawk finally.

''He had a great many enemies,'' said Bowman.

''Are you aware of the penalties for refusing to cooperate with the Guard during an investigation?'' asked Fisher.

''Of course,'' said Bowman. ''I am doing my best to

cooperate, Captain Fisher. I've answered every question you've asked me.''

''All right,'' said Hawk. ''That's all for now. Wait in the parlour with the others, and send in Dorimant.''

Bowman nodded briefly to them both, rose unhurriedly to his feet and left the library, closing the door quietly behind him.

''Politicians,'' said Hawk disgustedly. ''Getting answers to questions is like pulling teeth. The trouble is, technically he's in the right. He did answer all our questions; we just didn't know the right questions to ask him. We can't come flat out and accuse him of bedding his employer's wife. Firstly, he'd deny it anyway, and secondly, if by some chance we were wrong, he'd have us thrown out of the Guard.''

''Yeah,'' said Fisher. ''But there's no doubt in my mind. You saw them together—the way they were reacting to each other. It's as clear as the nose on his face. I can't believe Blackstone didn't know. Or at least suspect . . .''

Hawk shrugged. ''You heard Visage; perhaps he chose not to know. He couldn't risk a divorce, and Bowman was useful to him. . . .''

''Only as long as Bowman was discreet about it, and in my experience, he's not very subtle when it comes to approaching women.''

Hawk looked at her sharply. ''Oh, yes? Do I take it he approached you somewhen this evening?''

''Yes. I took care of it. I explained that I wasn't interested, and he went away.''

''Just like that?''

''Pretty much. Oh, I explained that you'd kill him slowly and painfully, and I did have my knife pressed against his gut, but . . .''

"Yeah," said Hawk, grinning. "You've always been . . . persuasive, Isobel."

"Thank you. To get back to the subject. If Bowman had been indiscreet about his affair with Katherine, and Blackstone got to hear of it . . ."

"No man likes to believe the woman he loves doesn't love him anymore," said Hawk. "Older man, younger woman; it's an old story. But even if Katherine and Bowman were having an affair, it doesn't mean they committed the murder. It's not proof."

"No, but it is a motive. And Katherine was the one who came and told us that something must have happened to her husband. . . ."

There was a knock on the door, and Dorimant came in. He hesitated in the doorway a moment, as though unsure of his reception, and then stepped quickly into the library and shut the door behind him. Hawk nodded curtly at the empty chair, and Dorimant came forward and sank into it. His face was pale and drawn, and his movements were clumsy, as though some of the strength had gone out of him. But when he finally raised his head to look at Hawk, his mouth was firm and his eyes didn't waver.

"Did you have much luck with Bowman?" he asked quietly.

"Some," said Hawk.

Dorimant smiled harshly. "I'd lay good odds he's already told you one lie. You asked him where he was at the time of the murder, and he said alone in his room. Right? I thought so. He wasn't alone. I saw Katherine go into his room, just after we all came upstairs to change. I was just leaving the bathroom. She didn't see me."

"Thank you for telling us," said Fisher. "We'll bear it in mind. Now, sir Dorimant, where were you at the time of the murder?"

"In my room."

"Alone?"

"No. Visage was with me."

Hawk raised an eyebrow. "Now, that's strange," he said slowly. "She told us she was in her room, alone. Why should she lie to us about that?"

"She wants to protect me," said Dorimant, looking at his hands. "I'm currently separated from my wife, but not yet divorced. The separation is far from amicable, and my dear wife would just love to find some scandal she could use as ammunition against me."

"So why are you telling us?" said Fisher.

"To prove I've nothing to hide."

"You were Blackstone's political adviser," said Hawk. "I've heard a lot about Blackstone's enemies, but so far nobody seems ready to actually name them. How about you?"

Dorimant shrugged. "It's no secret, Captain Hawk. There's Geoffrey Tobias; he used to represent the Heights in Council before William took his seat away from him at the last election. Then there's the DeWitt brothers; they stand to lose a lot of money if William's bill becomes law. They own property down in the docks. It's in a foul state, and they've neither the money nor the inclination to make the repairs the bill will require. There's Hugh Carnell, the leading conservative on the Council; old and mean and hates change in general and William's changes in particular. I could go on, but why bother? You said yourself earlier on that no one could have got into the house to kill William. The murderer has to be one of us."

"That's true," said Hawk. "But someone here could be in the pay of one of those enemies."

"It's possible, I suppose," said Dorimant. He didn't sound too convinced.

"Let's talk about Katherine and Bowman," said Fisher. "Do you think they're capable of murder?"

"We're all capable of murder," said Dorimant. "Providing we're pushed hard enough by something we want, or fear. Edward Bowman has had years of being second-in-command to William, and he's always been ambitious. And he knew Katherine would never leave William. She liked the money and the prestige too much, and in her own way, she was always fond of William. Even though she was cheating on him."

"Let us suppose for a moment," said Hawk, "that Bowman did kill Blackstone. Would Katherine have supported him in that, or would he have to do it on his own, and hope she never found out he was responsible?"

"I don't know." Dorimant shrugged angrily. "I'm not a mind reader. People can do strange things when they're in love."

"What about the other guests?" said Fisher. "Is there anyone else in this house with a motive to kill Blackstone?"

"I don't know about motives," said Dorimant slowly. "I know William had quarrelled recently with Adam Stalker."

"Really?" said Hawk. "That's interesting. What did they quarrel about?"

"I don't know. I don't think anybody knows. Neither of them would talk about it. But it must have been pretty serious. William was very angry about it; I could tell."

"Anything else you can tell us?" said Fisher.

"Not really. We all admired William; we all believed in him. And most of us liked him."

"How did you feel about him?" said Fisher.

Dorimant looked at her steadily. "William Blackstone was the bravest and finest man I ever met."

"Thank you," said Hawk. "That will be all for the moment. Please wait in the parlour with the others, and send in Katherine Blackstone."

Dorimant nodded and got to his feet. He left without looking back.

"He seemed very eager to lay the blame on Bowman," said Hawk slowly. "Almost too eager."

"Yeah," said Fisher. "I don't know about you, Hawk, but my head hurts. The more people we see, the more complicated and impossible this case gets. We've got more suspects than we can shake a stick at, and we still haven't got a clue as to how the murder was committed!"

"Stay with it, lass," said Hawk, smiling in spite of himself. "After all, we've both had experience with Court intrigues in the past, and if we can handle that, we can certainly handle this. Let's face it. Compared to some courtiers we've known, these people are amateurs. Now, how do you feel about Dorimant? He seemed sincere enough."

"Yeah," said Fisher. "But we've only his word that Visage was with him at the time of the murder. He could be lying."

"It's possible. But then again, it's not the kind of thing you'd expect him to admit if it wasn't true."

"Right." Fisher frowned thoughtfully. "And if Dorimant and Visage are having an affair, that takes away Visage's motivation, doesn't it? I mean, she couldn't be having an affair with Dorimant *and* Blackstone. Could she?"

"It does seem rather unlikely," said Hawk, "but we don't know that Visage and Dorimant were having an affair. All right, they were both in his room, but Dorimant never actually said why. Perhaps they had some other reason for being there. . . ."

Fisher groaned. ''My head's starting to hurt again. . . .''

The door opened and Katherine Blackstone came in. She looked pale but composed. She shut the door carefully behind her and glanced quickly round the library, as though searching for some hidden listener. She looked steadily at Hawk and Fisher, and then sank gracefully into the chair before them.

''Well?'' she said harshly. ''Who killed my husband?''

''We're still working on it,'' said Hawk politely. ''Detective work is a slow process, but we usually get there in the end. There are a few questions we need to ask you.''

''All right. Go ahead.''

''Let's start with the events leading up to the murder. You and your husband went upstairs to change for dinner. He went into the bedroom and you went to the bathroom. You came back, and found the door to your room locked. You called to your husband, but couldn't get any reply. You became worried, and went downstairs to fetch Fisher and myself. We went back with you, broke the door in, and found your husband dead. Is that correct?''

''Yes. That's what happened.''

''Is there anything missing from that account?''

''No.''

''Did anyone see you, or talk to you, on the landing?''

''No.''

''It has been suggested,'' said Fisher carefully, ''that you visited Edward Bowman in his room.''

''That's a lie,'' said Katherine flatly. ''I suppose you've also been told that we're having an affair? I thought so. William's enemies have been trying to use that slander against him for years. Who said it this time? Graham? No, he's too loyal to William. Visage. I'll bet it was that simpering bitch Visage. She always had eyes for William, but he hardly even knew she existed. Edward and I have been friends for a long time, but never more than that. I loved my husband, and no one else. And now he's dead, all his enemies will come crawling out of their holes to try and blacken his reputation with the same old lies, in the hope they can destroy what he achieved!''

"Who do you think killed him?" asked Fisher.

"I don't know." Katherine suddenly seemed very tired, as though all the defiance had gone out of her along with her angry words. She sat slumped in her chair, her eyes vague and far away. "I can't think straight anymore. William had any number of enemies."

"Had he quarrelled with anyone recently?" asked Fisher.

Katherine shrugged. "Not that I know of. I know he wasn't too pleased with Adam about something, but it couldn't have been that important. William never said anything about it to me."

"Who actually invited Stalker to this party?" asked Fisher.

"I did," said Katherine. "William didn't bother himself with minor matters like that. But he knew Adam would be here. If we hadn't invited him, it would have been a frightful snub."

"Thank you," said Hawk. 'I think that's all for now. Please wait with the others in the parlour, and ask Lord Hightower to come in."

"Is that it?" said Katherine. "Is that all you wanted to ask me?"

"For the moment," said Fisher. "There might be a few more questions later."

Katherine Blackstone nodded slowly, and got up out of her chair. "Find my husband's killer," she said softly. "I don't care how you do it, but find him.'' She left the library without looking back.

Hawk scowled unhappily. ''If she is lying, she's a very good liar.''

''From what I've heard, she was the finest actress in all Haven,'' said Fisher. ''In her day. She might be a little rusty after so long away from the stage, but a few lies with a straight face shouldn't be beyond her abilities.''

''But what if she is telling the truth?'' said Hawk. ''Dorimant could have his own reasons for lying.''

''Yes,'' said Fisher. ''He could. But one of the unpleasant truths of murder is that when a man or woman meets a violent end, the wife or the husband is usually the most likely suspect. Katherine could have good reasons for wanting her husband dead. Blackstone might have overlooked his wife's infidelity in the past rather than risk damaging his political career with a scandal, but if the affair got too blatant he'd have to divorce her, or lose all respect. You heard what Dorimant said. Katherine was fond of her husband, but she loved the money and prestige of being a Councillor's wife. As his widow, she could have the money and the prestige, and her lover as well.''

''Right,'' said Hawk. ''And there's a few holes in her story, as well. According to her, she went upstairs, went to the bathroom, came back and found the door locked, and then came down to us. And as you said, between her going up and coming down again there had to be a gap of about twenty minutes. That's a long time in the bathroom . . . And—if she did bang on the locked door and call out to her husband—how is it that no one else heard her? No one else has mentioned hearing her call out. You'd have thought someone would come out to see what was happening. . . .''

''Yeah,'' said Fisher. ''Mind you, if you're looking for

another front-runner, the one thing that practically every-one agrees on is that Blackstone had a big row with Adam Stalker not long ago.''

"Now that is pushing it," said Hawk. "Adam Stalk-er . . . ?''

The library door suddenly flew open, and Lord and Lady Hightower strode in. Lord Roderik slammed the door shut, and he and his wife stood together facing Hawk and Fisher. Their expressions were openly defiant.

"I asked to see you alone, my Lord," said Hawk.

"I don't give a damn what you asked for," said High-tower. "There's nothing you could possibly have to say to me that can't be said in front of my wife.''

"Very well," said Hawk. "Where were you at the time of the murder, my Lord?''

"In my room. With my wife.''

"Is that right, my Lady?" asked Fisher.

"Of course," said the Lady Elaine, disdainfully.

"Thank you," said Hawk. "That will be all for the moment, my Lord and Lady.''

Hightower looked startled for a moment, and then his face was hard and unyielding again. "I demand to know why I was prevented from examining the body. What are you trying to hide from us?''

"I said that will be all, my Lord," said Hawk politely. "You may rejoin the others in the parlour. And ask Adam Stalker to come in, if you please.''

Hightower glared at him. Hawk met his gaze calmly, and after a moment Hightower turned away. He took his wife by the arm, opened the door for her and led her out. He slammed the door shut behind him, and the sound echoed loudly in the small room. Fisher looked at Hawk.

"That's all? What about all the other questions we should have asked them?''

"What was the point?" said Hawk. "They've got each other as an alibi, and Hightower isn't going to volunteer any information to the likes of us. Whatever we ask, he'll just say it's none of our business. If he has anything to say, he'll save it for our superiors tomorrow. He wants us to fail, lass. That way he can prove to himself that his son's death was my fault after all."

"He'd actually risk his friend's murderer getting away?"

"He knows there'll be a full forensic team in here tomorrow, once the isolation spell is down and we can file our report. He'll talk to them if he's got anything to say, which I doubt."

Fisher frowned. "The law is on our side. We could compel him to talk."

"I don't think so. Hightower's an important man in this city. He may no longer be Chief Commander, but he still has influential friends. No, Isobel, anything we learn about Hightower will have to come from other people. He wouldn't give us the time of day if we held a sword to his throat."

Fisher shrugged unhappily. "I suppose you're right. The Lady Elaine might not be such a tough nut, though. I'll see if I can get her on her own, later. I might get some information out of her, woman to woman."

"Worth a try," said Hawk. "But don't raise your hopes too high."

The door swung open, and Stalker stood framed in the doorway. He held the pose a moment, and then entered the library, ducking his head slightly to avoid banging it on the doorframe. He sat down facing Hawk and Fisher, and the chair creaked loudly under his weight. Even sitting down, Stalker was still a head taller than Hawk or Fisher.

"All right," said Stalker grimly. "You've talked to everyone else and heard their stories. Who killed William?"

"It's too early to say, yet," said Hawk.

"You must have learned something!"

"Yes," said Hawk. "Most of it contradictory. Where were you at the time of the murder, sir Stalker?"

"In my room. Alone. I don't have any witnesses, or an alibi. But I didn't kill William."

"Is there any reason why we should think you did?" asked Fisher.

Stalker smiled briefly. "Someone must have told you by now that William and I hadn't been getting on too well of late."

"There was some talk that the two of you had argued about something," said Hawk.

"We'd decided to go our separate ways," said Stalker. "William was always too slow, too cautious, for me. I wanted to get out there and do things, change things. William and I were always arguing, right from the start. We both wanted the same things, more or less, but we could never agree on the best way to achieve them. Looking back, it's a wonder we stayed together as long as we did. Anyway, I finally decided to go off on my own, and see what my reputation could do for me at the next election. I think I'll make a pretty good Councillor, myself. Haven could do a lot worse. It often has, in the past. But that's all there was to our quarrel—just a parting of the ways. I had nothing against the man; I admired him, always have. Straightest man I ever met."

"So who do you think killed Councillor Blackstone?" said Fisher.

Stalker looked at her pityingly. "Isn't it obvious? William died alone, in a room locked from the inside. Sorcery. Has to be."

"Gaunt doesn't think so," said Hawk.

Stalker shrugged. "I wouldn't trust him further than I could throw him. Never trust a sorcerer."

"How long had you known Blackstone?" asked Fisher.

Stalker stirred restlessly in his chair and glanced irritably at Fisher. "Not long. Two years, maybe."

"Apart from the sorcerer," said Hawk, "can you think of anyone with a reason for wanting Blackstone dead?"

Stalker smiled sourly. "I suppose you've heard about Katherine and Edward?"

"Yes," said Fisher. "Is it true?"

"I don't know. Maybe. Women are fickle creatures. No offence intended."

"What about political enemies?" said Hawk quickly.

"He had his share. No one in particular, though."

"I see," said Hawk. "Thank you, sir Stalker. That will be all for now. If you'd care to wait with the others in the parlour, my partner and I will join you in a while. By the way, I gave orders that no one was to go near the body. Perhaps you could remind the others, and make it clear to them that I meant it. . . ."

"Of course," said Stalker. "Glad to be of help, Captain Hawk." He nodded briefly to Fisher, got up and left the library. Hawk and Fisher sat in silence a while, staring at nothing and thinking furiously.

"You know," said Fisher, "I think things were less complicated before we started asking questions."

Hawk laughed briefly. "You could be right, lass. Let's try and sort out the wheat from the chaff. What actual suspects have we got? It seems to me that Katherine Blackstone heads the list, with Bowman a close second. Either separately or together, they had good reason to want Blackstone dead. Assuming they were having an affair. Unfortunately, we don't have any real evidence that they were. Gossip isn't evidence."

"Dorimant said he saw Katherine going into Bowman's room," said Fisher. "But Dorimant could have his own reasons for lying. Which leaves us right back where we started. So, who else can we point the finger at? I think Gaunt has to be a suspect, if only because at the moment he's the only one who could have committed the murder."

"On the other hand," said Hawk, "he couldn't have used sorcery to get into the room without Visage knowing."

"She did say she was nowhere near as powerful as Gaunt."

"True. And just maybe they were working together."

"No, Hawk, I still don't buy that. You saw the witch when she was talking about Blackstone; she all but worshipped the ground he trod on."

Hawk frowned. "That kind of worship can be dangerous. If something happened to disillusion her, and that worship turned sour . . ."

"Yeah," said Fisher reluctantly. "You're right, Hawk. Visage has to be a suspect."

"Ah, hell," said Hawk tiredly. "Until we've got something definite to go on, they're all suspects."

"Including Stalker?"

"I don't know, lass. Adam Stalker is a hero and a legend . . . but like Dorimant said, we're all capable of murder if we're pushed hard enough. And Stalker was definitely jumpy all the time we were talking to him."

"So we count him as a suspect?"

"Yes," said Hawk. "He's killed often enough in the past, with good reason. Maybe this time he found a bad reason." He sighed wearily, and stretched out his legs before him. "I think we've done all we can, for the moment. Gaunt's isolation spell won't wear off until first light, so we're all stuck here for the night anyway. Let's call it a day, and yell for some help in the morning. A forensic magician should get us some answers, even if he has to set up a truthspell to do it.''

"Gaunt could set up a truthspell," said Fisher thoughtfully.

"Yeah, I suppose he could, but we don't have the authority to order everyone to submit to it, and somehow I don't see them volunteering. There are some powerful people out there, Isobel. We're going to need some pretty solid backing before we can start pushing them around.''

"Right," said Fisher. "Come on, let's get out of here. The sooner we face our jovial bunch of suspects, the sooner we can pack them all off to bed, and then maybe we can get a little peace and quiet.''

Hawk nodded tiredly, and he and Fisher got to their feet. Fisher started towards the door, and then stopped as she realised Hawk wasn't with her. He was standing still in the middle of the room, head cocked to one side, listening.

"What is it?" said Fisher.

"I'm not sure," said Hawk slowly. "I thought I heard something. Something . . . strange.'' He looked about him, frowning, and then his gaze fell on the closed door to his left.

"Forget it, Hawk," said Fisher quickly. "That's Gaunt's laboratory. It's private, and it's locked.''

"Yeah," said Hawk. "And Visage said she found it . . . disturbing.''

He moved quietly over to the door and pressed his ear against the wood. Fisher glanced quickly about her, and then moved over to stand beside him.

"Can you hear anything?" she asked quietly.

"No.''

"What did you think you heard?''

"I'm not sure." Hawk straightened up and stepped back from the door. He frowned, and looked thoughtfully at the door handle. "It sounded like a growl, or something. . . ." He tried the handle cautiously. It turned easily in his grasp, but the door wouldn't open. He let go of the handle.

"Hawk," said Fisher slowly, "there's something strange about that door. . . . I'm getting a very bad feeling about it. Come away."

"Nothing to worry about, lass. The door's locked."

"I don't care. Come away."

Hawk nodded stiffly. He could feel the hackles rising on the back of his neck. Whatever it was he'd heard, it was gone, but still he knew, with absolute certainty, that there was something awful on the other side of the laboratory door. Something that was listening, and waiting for him to open the door . . . He stepped back a pace and the feeling was gone. He swallowed dryly, and looked away.

"I suppose you're bound to come across a few strange things in a sorcerer's house," he said slowly. "Let's get out of here."

"Right," said Fisher.

Hawk moved over to the main door, pulled it open and walked quickly out into the hall. Fisher stayed close behind him all the way, her hand on the pommel of her sword. Once out in the hall, they both felt a little ridiculous. Hawk shook himself quickly and pulled the library door shut. When he had a moment, he'd better have a word with Gaunt about his laboratory. . . . He glanced at Fisher, and she nodded quickly. Hawk smiled wryly, and then walked confidently forward into the parlour, with Fisher at his side. The sorcerer and his guests looked at the Guards with a thinly disguised mixture of politeness and hostility.

"Thank you for your patience," said Hawk. "This part of the investigation is at an end. Everything else will have to wait until we can bring in the experts tomorrow morning."

Bowman stepped forward a pace. "Gaunt tells us we can't leave the house till morning, because of the isolation spell. Did you order him to cast that spell?"

"Yes," said Hawk. "I couldn't take the risk of the killer getting away, and I had no other means of ensuring that he couldn't leave the house."

"But that means we're all stuck here!"

"That's right," said Hawk. "I suggest you retire to your rooms and get what sleep you can."

"Are you saying," said Hightower slowly, "that because of you we have to spend the night here, when one of us may be a killer?"

"You can always lock your door," said Fisher.

"That didn't save William," said Dorimant.

"All right," said Hawk sharply. "That's enough. It's not a happy situation, I know, but there's nothing we can do about it. If you've got any complaints, you can take them up with my superiors in the morning. In the meantime, I don't think any of us are in any real danger as long as we act sensibly. I suggest you all go to your rooms and stay there. Fisher and I will be here in the parlour all night, on guard. If anyone feels at all worried, they have only to call out and we'll be there in the time it takes to run up the stairs. If anyone starts moving about, we'll know. So I suggest that once you're in your room, you stay there."

"What if I want to go to the bathroom?" asked Bowman.

"Use the pot under your bed," said Fisher.

There was a slight pause as the guests looked at each

other uncertainly. Then Katherine made for the door and
the group broke apart. There was a muttering of good
nights, and one by one the guests left the parlour and made
their way up the stairs to their rooms. Hawk signalled for
Gaunt to stay behind, and the sorcerer did so. When everyone else had gone, Hawk and Fisher looked steadily at
the sorcerer.

"What have you got in your laboratory, sir Gaunt?"
said Hawk bluntly.

"Odds and ends. Chemicals and the like. Why?"

Hawk scowled uncertainly. "I felt something . . .
something strange. . . ."

"Oh, of course," said Gaunt, smiling slightly. "I
should have warned you. The door has an avoidance spell
on it, as a precaution. If you get too close to it, the spell
makes you feel so uncomfortable and worried that you
daren't try to force open the door. Simple, but effective."

"Ah, I see," said Hawk, trying not to sound too re-
lieved. "Well, sir sorcerer, I think that's all. Fisher and I
will spend the night here in the parlour. One of us will
always be on watch."

"That sounds very reassuring," said Gaunt. "I'll be
sleeping in my laboratory tonight. If you need me for any
reason, just call. I'll hear you. Well, I'll see you both in
the morning. Good night, Captain Hawk, Captain Fisher."

He bowed politely, and left the parlour. Hawk and Fisher
looked round the empty room.

"We never did get our dinner," said Fisher.

"Yeah," said Hawk. "It's a tough life in the Guard."

"Toss you for the first watch?"

"Your coin or mine?"

"How well you know me," said Fisher, grinning.

4

Secrets

Edward Bowman sat back in the chair by his bed and looked round the room Gaunt had given him. It was a comfortable enough room, all told, but the color scheme was a dark, disturbing shade of mauve. It looked like the room had died. Bowman wondered vaguely why the sorcerer should have chosen such an unrelentingly repulsive décor. The man usually showed such excellent taste. On the other hand, Gaunt hardly ever used these rooms. Maybe he'd inherited the décor from the old days, when the house still belonged to the DeFerrier family. Now that was a definite possibility. The DeFerriers had always been . . . strange. Bowman looked again at the clock on the mantelpiece. The clock had a loud aggressive tick, but its hands seemed to crawl round the dial. Bowman stirred impatiently in his chair. He'd wait another three quarters of an hour, to be sure everyone was asleep, and then, finally, he could go and see Katherine.

He frowned thoughtfully. Katherine had taken the death of her husband pretty badly. He'd known she was still fond of William, even though their marriage had fallen apart, but he'd still been surprised at how upset she'd been. . . . He wondered if she'd have taken the news of his death as badly. Bowman shook his head irritably. He hadn't been jealous of William when he was alive, and he wasn't going to start now the man was dead. Katherine was his, just as she'd always been his. He'd go and see her in a while, and hold her in his arms, and everything would be fine again. Another three quarters of an hour . . . He'd have to be careful, though, or Hawk and Fisher might hear him. And that might prove rather embarrassing.

Hawk and Fisher . . . Bowman's mouth tightened. They were going to be a nuisance; he could tell. Damn their impertinence! Of all the Guards Dorimant could have chosen as William's bodyguards, he had to pick those two—the only really honest Guards in the city. Anyone else would have had enough sense to ask a few polite questions, and then step aside and let their superiors take over—men who understood the political considerations. But not these two. They didn't seem to care how much dirt they stirred up, or who got hurt in the process. All right, finding William's killer was important, but the cause for which William had stood was more important. A scandal now could set Reform back a dozen years.

Bowman scowled thoughtfully. Maybe he shouldn't have tried to chat up Captain Fisher after all. It had seemed like a good idea at the time. It would draw attention away from him and Katherine, and besides, he'd always had a thing about tall blondes. . . . But now he was a murder suspect, and one of the investigating officers had a grudge against him. Great. Just what he needed.

His scowl deepened as he tried to think which ranking officers in the Guard owed him a favor or two. There had to be someone; there was always *someone*. He finally shook his head and gave up. It was late and he was tired;

he couldn't even think straight anymore. Besides, pulling strings was the last resort. It might not even come to that. As long as he and Katherine kept their mouths shut and brazened it out, no one could prove anything. Let people think what they liked; without proof they wouldn't dare say anything.

Bowman looked at the clock again. He'd better not stay long with Katherine tonight. He'd have to get some sleep if he was to get any work done tomorrow. And there was a hell of a lot to be done. With William dead, Reform could lose the whole Heights area if someone didn't step into the breach pretty damned quick. Tobias had never made any bones about wanting his old seat on the Council back, and with William's last bill still hanging in the balance . . . There were a great many pressure groups with an interest in that bill, and together they could make or break the man who took over from William. Bowman shook his head angrily. Whatever else happened, Tobias had to be kept out of the Council. All on his own that scheming hypocritical crook could undo everything Reform had achieved so far. Someone would have to stand against him at the next election. And who better than William Blackstone's loyal and faithful right-hand man?

But he couldn't just stand up and announce his candidacy. That would look bad, so soon after William's death. No, he'd need someone else, to suggest him. Someone like Katherine, perhaps. Only that might look bad, too. . . . He smiled, and shook his head. There had to be a way. There was always a way, if you looked hard enough.

He leaned back in his chair, and carefully didn't look at the clock again. He could be patient, when he had to. He'd learned a lot about patience during his long years as William's right-hand man. Bowman frowned thoughtfully. It was going to feel strange, working without William.

They'd been partners for so long . . . but now, finally, he
had his own chance to be the front-runner, and that felt
very good. It was a shame about William's death, but then,
life goes on. . . . He thought about Katherine, waiting for
him to come to her, and smiled.

Life goes on.

Adam Stalker slowly pulled off his shirt and dropped it on
the chair by his bed. He was tired, and his back ached
unmercifully. He sat on the edge of the bed, and felt it
give perceptibly under his weight. Damn thing was too
soft for his liking. He preferred a hard support for his
back. The room was hot and muggy with the shutters
closed, but he knew better than to try and open them.
Gaunt would have fixed them not to open. The sorcerer
worried about assassins. Stalker stretched slowly and
looked down at himself. His frame was still muscular,
his stomach still flat and hard, but the scars depressed
him. The thin white lines sprawled across his chest and gut,
digging pale furrows in his tan, crossing and recrossing, and
finally spilling down his arms. There were more on his back.
Stalker hated them. Each and every one was a constant re-
minder of how close he'd come to dying. Each scar was a
wound that might have killed him if he'd been a little slower
or a little less lucky. Stalker hated reminders of his own
mortality.

He looked round the room Gaunt had given him. Not
bad. The dull red color scheme looked grim and disturbing
in the light from the single candle, but he didn't mind.
He'd known worse in his time, in his travels. He lay back
on his bed and stretched out, without bothering to remove
his trousers or his boots. It wouldn't be the first time he'd
slept in his clothes; he'd done it often enough in the past,
out in the wilds. And he was tired. Very tired. It had been

a long hard day. . . . He stared drowsily at the ceiling, letting his mind drift where it would. Hawk and Fisher . . . the Guards. A good team. They worked well together, and from what he'd heard, they'd done a good job on the Chandler Lane vampire. He sighed wistfully. Staking vampires . . . that was real work for a man. Not like all this standing around at political meetings he'd had to get used to. Politics . . . He'd rather face a vampire than another committee. Maybe he should take a break for a while; get out of the city and back into the open lands, into the wilder areas where he belonged.

Stalker frowned, and grimaced resignedly. No, that was a younger man talking. Those days were over for him. Sleeping in the rough would play hell with his back, even in this weather. Besides, he had a real chance of taking William's place as the official Reform candidate at the next election, if he played his cards right. It shouldn't be too difficult. With his name and reputation, the opposition wouldn't stand a chance. Stalker yawned widely, and wriggled himself into a more comfortable position. If he was going to take over William's place, he'd better start talking to the right people. Not too soon; that would look bad. But leave it too late, and other people might get in ahead of him. He'd start with Katherine. . . . She'd need some support in the next few months. Though she'd probably be getting enough of that from Bowman. Stalker's lip curled. William should have done something about that, not let it go dragging on. A man looks after what's his, no matter what. William should have been tougher with her, knocked some sense into her, made it clear who wore the trousers. Stalker sighed. He'd been tempted to do something about Bowman himself, but he never had. Never interfere in other people's domestic problems. He'd learned that the hard way.

Still, Katherine was going to need him a damn sight
more than she would Bowman, for the time being at least.
Things were liable to get a bit rough, once the various
factions in the Council learned of William's death. And
you could bet there'd be factions jostling for position within
the Reform cause, as well. Katherine was going to need a
bodyguard. Stalker smiled sourly. Bowman might fancy
himself a duellist, but he'd be damn-all use in a back-alley
brawl. And Visage might be good at fending off magic,
but she'd be no use at all when it came to stopping a
dagger thrown from a crowd. No, Katherine was going to
need him for a while yet. And he could make good use of
her. . . .

Unless she decided to go into politics herself. Stalker
scowled. She just might; women didn't seem to know their
place anymore. That Captain Fisher might look and talk
tough, but she'd probably fold in a minute when the going
got really hard. Women always did.

Stalker stirred restlessly. The room was swelteringly hot,
and he thought seriously about trying to open the shutters.
He finally decided against it. Knowing Gaunt, even if he
could get the shutters open, he'd probably set off an alarm
or something. The whole house was crawling with sorcery. Stalker sneered silently. Magic . . . He never did
trust sorcerers. A man should make his way in the world,
with courage and a sword, not by hiding away in stuffy
rooms, poring over old books and making nasty smells
with chemicals. All of Gaunt's so-called power hadn't been
enough to protect William.

Stalker sighed. If only he and William hadn't quarrelled
. . . so many things might have been different.

If only . . . the most futile phrase in the language.
Stalker looked up at the ceiling, mostly hidden in the
gloom. It had been a long time since he'd last slept under

this roof, in this room. Must be all of thirty years, and more. He wondered if Gaunt knew this had once been his bedroom, when he was a boy. Probably not. Just one of life's little ironies no doubt. There was no one left now who knew that Adam Stalker had been born a DeFerrier, and that this house had once been his home. Until he ran away, sickened at what his family had become. They were all dead now; parents, brothers, sisters, aunts and uncles. All gone. The DeFerriers were no more, and Adam Stalker was happy with the name he had made for himself.

He closed his eyes and breathed deeply. Get some sleep. There was a lot to be done, come the morning.

Graham Dorimant paced up and down in his room, and wondered what to do for the best. William was dead, and the Guards were no nearer finding his killer. And all too soon that slimy little creep Bowman would be angling for William's seat in Council. The man was barely cold, and already the vultures were gathering. All right, somebody had to take his place, but it didn't have to be Bowman. And it wouldn't be, as long as Dorimant had any say in the matter.

He stopped pacing, and frowned thoughtfully. There was no guarantee it would be any of his business. He'd worked for William, and William was dead. Katherine might well decide she had no more use for him, and bring in her own advisers. Dorimant bit his lip uncertainly. Losing the job wasn't in itself a problem; even after his divorce he should have more than enough money left to last him out. But to give up the excitement of politics, to go back to the empty-headed social whirl of endless parties at fashionable places, the childish fads and games and intrigues . . .

Maybe Lord Hightower could offer him some kind of position; the old man wanted to get more deeply involved

in politics, and he'd need an adviser he could trust. . . .
Yes. That might be it. Lord Roderik wasn't anything like
the man William had been, but he was honest and sincere,
and that was rare enough these days. He'd have a word
with Hightower in the morning. Assuming William's killer
didn't strike again, and murder everyone in their beds.
Dorimant glanced nervously at his door. It was securely
locked and bolted, with a chair jammed up against it for
good measure. He was safe enough. The two Guards were
just downstairs, keeping watch. After the Chandler Lane
business a simple assassin shouldn't give them too much
trouble.

He frowned uncertainly. Maybe he should have told
them about Visage, and what she'd seen. He'd wanted to,
but she had begged him not to. Now both he and she were
in the position of having lied to the Guard. If they ever
found out . . . He remembered Hawk's cold, scarred face,
and shivered suddenly. He didn't care, he told himself de-
fiantly. He'd done the right thing. Visage had come to him
for help, and he had given it. Nothing else mattered.

He hadn't realised before just how important Visage was
to him.

He sighed, and sank into the chair by the bed. He knew
he ought to go to bed and get some rest, but he wasn't
sleepy. It was hard for him to believe that William was
really gone. He'd admired the man for so long, and been
his friend for such a short time. . . . And now, here he
was helping to conceal evidence that might help find William's killer.

*I'm sorry, William. But I think I love her, and I can't
risk her being hurt.*

Lord and Lady Hightower got ready for bed in silence.
Lord Roderik sat in the chair by the bed and watched his

wife brush her hair before the dressing table mirror. When fully unbound, her long white hair hung halfway down her back. Roderik had always liked to watch her brush her hair, a simple intimate moment she shared with no one but him. He wondered wistfully when her hair had turned white. He couldn't remember. When they were first married her hair had been a beautiful shade of honey yellow, but that had been long ago, when he was still a Captain. With something like shock, Roderik realised that that had been almost thirty years ago. Thirty years . . . Where had the time gone?

Elaine looked into the mirror and caught him watching her. She smiled, but he looked quickly away. She put down her brush, and turned around to face him. She was wearing the white silk nightdress he'd bought her for her last birthday. She looked very lovely, and very defenceless.

Don't ask me, Elaine. Please. I can't tell you. I can't tell anyone. . . .

"What is it, Rod?" she said quietly. "Something's been bothering you for months now. Why won't you tell me about it?"

"Nothing to tell," said Roderik gruffly.

"Bull," said his wife. "I haven't known you all these years without being able to tell when something's gnawing at you. Is it Paul? I thought you were finally getting over his death. You should never have gone off on those stupid campaigns, the werewolf hunts. I should never have let you go."

"They helped. . . ."

"Did they? Every time some fool jumped at his own shadow and shouted 'werewolf!' you went racing off to track it down. And how many did you find, out of all those dozens of hunts? One. Just one. That was why the King made you resign, wasn't it? Not just because you'd reached the retirement age, but because you were never there when he needed you!''

''Don't,'' whispered Roderik, squeezing his eyes shut. Elaine rose quickly out of her chair and hurried over to kneel beside him. She put a hand on his arm, and he reached blindly across to squeeze it tightly.

''It's all right, my dear,'' said Elaine softly. ''I'm not angry with you, I'm just worried. Worried about you. You've been so . . . different lately.''

''Different?'' Roderik opened his eyes and looked at her uncertainly. ''How do you mean, different?''

''Oh, I don't know; moody, irritable, easily upset. I'm not blind, you know. And there've been other things. . . .''

''Elaine . . .''

''Once a month, you go off on your own. You don't come back for days on end, and when you do, you won't tell me where you've been or what you've been doing.''

''I have my reasons,'' said Roderik gruffly.

''Yes,'' said Elaine, ''I think you do. You mustn't feel badly about it, Rod. When a man gets to your age I know that sometimes they, well, start to feel insecure about . . . themselves. I just want you to know that I don't mind, as long as you come home to me.''

''You don't mind?'' said Roderik slowly. ''Elaine, what are you talking about?''

''I don't mind that you have another woman,'' said Elaine steadily. ''You shouldn't look so astonished, my dear. It wasn't that difficult to work out. You have a mistress. It really doesn't matter.''

Roderik stood up, took his wife by the shoulders and made her stand up, facing him. He tried to say something, and couldn't. He took her in his arms and held her tightly. ''Elaine, my dear, my love. I promise you I don't have another woman. You're the only woman I ever wanted, the only woman I've ever loved. I promise you; there's never been anyone in my life but you, and there never will be.''

"Then where have you been going all these months?''

Roderik sighed, and held her away from him so that he could look at her. "I can't tell you, Elaine. Just believe me when I say I don't go because I want to, I go because I have to. It's important.''

"You mean it's . . . political?''

"In a way. I can't talk about it, Elaine. I can't.''

"Very well, my dear.'' Elaine leaned forward and kissed him on the cheek. "Tell me about it when you can. Now let's go to bed. It's been a long day.''

"I think I'll sit up for a while. I'm not sleepy. You go to bed. I won't be long.''

Elaine nodded, and turned away to pull back the sheet. She didn't see the tears that glistened in Roderik's eyes for a moment. When she looked at him again, having first settled herself comfortably in bed, he was sitting on the chair, staring at nothing.

"Rod . . .''

"Yes?''

"Who do you think killed William?''

"I don't know. I can't even see how he was killed, never mind who or why.''

"Are we in any danger?''

"I shouldn't think so. Gaunt is on guard now; nothing will get by him. And there's always the two Guards downstairs. They're proficient enough at the simple things, I suppose. There's nothing for you to worry about, my dear. Go to sleep.''

"Yes, Rod. Blow out the lamp when you come to bed.''

"Elaine . . .''

"Yes?''

"I love you. Whatever happens, never doubt that I love you."

The witch Visage lay in her bed and stared at the ceiling. She didn't really like the bed. It was very comfortable, but it was too big. She felt lost in it. She stirred restlessly under the single thin sheet covering her. She felt hot and clammy, but she didn't like to throw back the sheet, not in a stranger's house. She'd feel naked and defenceless. Not that she was in any danger. She'd locked the door and set the wards. No one and nothing could get to her now. She was safe.

But only for the moment. She'd worked for William Blackstone all her adult life, and she didn't know what would become of her now that he was dead. William had always been much more than an employer to her; he had been her god. He was wise and just, and he fought the forces of evil in Haven. He always knew what to do, and he was always right, and if he hardly ever noticed the quiet young witch at his side, well, that was only to be expected. He always had so many important things on his mind.

Graham Dorimant had noticed her. He was always kind to her, and said nice things, and noticed when she wore a new dress. Perhaps he would look after her and take care of her. It was a nice thought.

Visage thought of the two Guards who'd questioned her, and frowned. They'd been polite enough, she supposed, but they hadn't really liked her. She could tell. She could always tell. And Hawk, the one with the scars and the single cold eye . . . He frightened her. She didn't like to be frightened. Visage pouted unhappily in the darkness. She'd told the Guards about Katherine and Edward, but they hadn't believed her. Not really. But all they had to do was start digging, and they'd find out the truth. And then everyone would see what had really been going on.

If the truth was ever allowed to come out. Visage scowled. There were a great many people who wouldn't want the truth to get out. After all, it might taint William's memory. Well, she didn't want that, but she couldn't let Katherine and Edward get away with it. She couldn't let that happen. She wouldn't let that happen. They had murdered her William, and they would pay for it, one way or another. Her hand went to the bone amulet that hung on a silver chain around her neck. She might be only a witch, but she had power of her own, and she would use it if she had to. If there was no other way to get justice for William.

Visage sighed tiredly. Poor William. She would miss him very much. She'd followed him for so many years . . . and now she would have to find someone else to follow. Someone else to tell her what to do. She'd talk to Graham about it in the morning. He liked her. She could tell.

The sorcerer Gaunt lay on his bed, in his laboratory. The air was deliciously cool and fresh, the summer heat kept at bay by his spells. The room was brightly lit by half a dozen oil lamps. For many reasons, some of them practical, Gaunt felt uneasy about sleeping in the dark. He lay on his back and looked slowly round the familiar, crowded room, taking in the plain wooden benches and their alchemical equipment, the shelves of ingredients, all neatly stacked in their proper order. . . . Gaunt felt at home in the laboratory, in a way he never did anywhere else in the house. He didn't really like the house much, if truth be told, but he needed it. He needed the security and the privacy it gave him, even if he did tend to rattle around in it like a single seed in a pod. There were times when he was tempted to give in to Stalker and sell him the damn house, but he never did. He couldn't.

He put forth his mind and tested the wards in and around the house, like a spider testing the many strands of its web. Everything was peaceful, everything as it should be. All was quiet. Gaunt frowned slightly. It worried him that he still had no idea how William had died. It worried him even more that the killer had to be one of his guests. There was no way an assassin could have got past his defences without him knowing. And yet he'd known these people for years, known and trusted them. . . . It just didn't seem possible.

Gaunt sighed tiredly. Everyone had their secrets, their own hidden darkness. He of all people should know that.

"Darling . . ."

The voice was soft, husky, alluring. Gaunt swallowed dryly. Just the sound of her voice sent little thrills of pleasure through him, but he wouldn't look at her. He wouldn't.

"Why don't you call to me, darling? All you have to do is call, and I'll come to you. You'd like that, wouldn't you?"

He didn't answer. He was a sorcerer, and he was in control.

"Always the same. You want me, but you won't admit it. You desire me, but you fight against it. I can't think why. If you didn't want me, why did you summon me?"

"Because I was weak!" snapped Gaunt. "Because I was a fool."

"Because you were human," purred the voice. "Is that such a terrible thing to be? You are powerful, my sweet, very powerful, but you still have human needs and weaknesses. It's no shame to give in to them."

"Shame?" said Gaunt. "What would you know about shame?"

"Nothing. Nothing at all." The voice laughed softly, and Gaunt shivered at the sound of it. "Look at me, darling. Look at me."

Gaunt looked at the pentacle marked out on the floor on the far side of the laboratory. The blue chalk lines glowed faintly with their own eerie light. Inside the pentacle sat the succubus. She looked at Gaunt with jet black eyes, and smiled mockingly. She was naked, and heart-stoppingly beautiful. The succubus was five feet tall, with a disturbingly voluptuous figure and a rawboned sensual face. The lamplight glowed golden on her perfect skin. Two small horns rose up from her forehead, almost hidden among the great mane of jet black hair. She stretched languidly, still smiling, and Gaunt groaned softly as the old familiar longing began again, just as he'd known it would.

"Yes," said the succubus. "I am beautiful, aren't I? And I'm yours, any time you want me. All you have to do is call me, darling, and I'll come to you. All you have to do is call to me. . . ."

"Come to me," said Gaunt. "Come to me, damn you!"

The succubus laughed happily and rose to her feet in a single lithe movement. She stepped out of the pentacle, the blue chalk lines flaring up briefly as she crossed them, and strode unhurriedly over to the sorcerer's bed. She pulled back the single sheet and sank down beside him.

"Damn me, my darling? No. You're the one who's damned, sorcerer. And isn't it lovely?"

Gaunt took her in his arms, and the old sweet madness took him once again.

Katherine Blackstone sat in the chair by the bed and looked listlessly round the spare room that Gaunt had opened up for her. The air was close and dusty, and the bed hadn't been aired, but she didn't care. At least it was a fair distance away from the room where her husband had died; the room where the body still lay. . . .

The *body*. Not her husband, or her late husband, just the body. William was gone, and what was left behind didn't even have to be addressed by name.

Katherine looked at the bed beside her, and looked away. Sleep might help, but she couldn't seem to summon the energy to get up, get undressed, and go to bed. And anyway, if she waited long enough she was sure Edward would come to her. She'd thought he'd be here by now, but he was probably just being sensible. It wouldn't do for them to be caught together tonight, of all nights. He'd be here soon. Maybe then she'd know what to do, what to say, for the best. For the moment, all she wanted to do was sit where she was and do nothing. She'd been married less than seven years, and here she was a widow. Widow . . . There was a harsh finality to the word; that's all there is, there isn't going to be any more. It's over. Katherine's thoughts drifted back and forth, moving round the subject of her husband's death but unable to settle on it. It was impossible to think of the great William Blackstone being dead. He'd been such an important man; meant so much to so many people. Katherine wanted to cry. She might feel better if she could only cry. But all she had inside of her was tiredness.

How could he have done it? How could he have left her in this mess? How could William have killed himself?

The Guards thought it was murder. So did everyone else. Only she knew it was really suicide. The Guards were already looking for signs of guilt, for something they could use as a motive. She'd known they were bound to bring up Edward Bowman, so she'd met that attack as she always had, by throwing it back in their faces as a lie and defying them to prove otherwise. *It has been suggested to us* . . . Oh, yes, she'd just bet it had. That little bitch Visage wouldn't have waited long to start spreading the poison.

She and Edward would have to be very careful in the future. For a while, at least.

Hawk and Fisher sat stretched out in their comfortable chairs, facing the hall. They'd put out all the lamps save two, and the parlour was gloomy enough to be restful on the eyes while still leaving enough light to see by. The house was quiet, the air hot and stuffy. Hawk yawned widely.

"Don't," said Fisher. "You'll set me off."

"Sorry," said Hawk. "I can't sleep. Too much on my mind."

"All right, then; you stand watch and I'll get some sleep."

"Suits me," said Hawk. "I shouldn't think we'll have any more trouble tonight."

"You could be right," said Fisher, settling herself comfortably in her chair and wishing vaguely that she had a pillow. "Whoever killed Blackstone, it didn't have the look of a spur-of-the-moment decision. A lot of careful planning had to have gone into it. What we have to worry about now is whether the killer had a specific grudge against Blackstone, or if he's just the first in a series of victims."

"You know," said Hawk, "we can't even be sure that Blackstone was the intended victim. Maybe he just saw someone in the wrong place at the wrong time, and had to die because he was a witness. The killer might still be waiting for his chance at the real victim."

"Don't," said Fisher piteously. "Isn't the case complicated enough as it is?"

"Sorry," said Hawk. "Just thinking . . ."

"Have you had any more ideas on who the killer might be?"

"Nothing new. Bowman and Katherine Blackstone have to be the most obvious choices; they had the most to gain. But I keep coming back to *how* the murder was committed. There's something about that locked room that worries me. I can't quite figure out what it is, but something keeps nagging at me. . . . Ah, well, no doubt it'll come to me eventually."

"My head's starting to ache again," said Fisher. "I'm no good at problems. Never have been. You know, Hawk, what gets me is the casual way it was done. I mean, one minute we're all standing around in here, knocking back the fruit cordial and chatting away nineteen to the dozen, and the next minute everyone goes off to change and Blackstone is killed. If the killer was one of the people in this room, he must have cast-iron nerves."

"Right," said Hawk.

They sat together a while, listening to the quiet. The house creaked and groaned around them, settling itself as old houses will. The air was still and hot and heavy. Hawk dropped one hand onto the shaft of his axe, where it stood leaning against the side of his chair. There were too many things about this case he didn't like, too many things that didn't add up. And he had a strong feeling that the night still had a few more surprises up its sleeve.

Time passed, and silence spread through the old house. Everyone was either asleep or sitting quietly in their rooms, waiting for the morning. The hall and the landing were empty, and the shadows lay undisturbed. A door eased silently open, and Edward Bowman looked out onto the landing. A single oil lamp glowed dully halfway down the right-hand wall, shedding a soft orange light over the landing. There was no one else about, and Bowman relaxed a little. Not that it mattered if anyone did see him. He could always claim he was going to the bathroom, but why complicate matters? Besides, he didn't want to do anything that might draw the attention of the Guards. He stepped out onto the landing and closed his bedroom door quietly behind him. He waited a moment, listening, and then padded down the landing to Katherine's room. He tried the door handle, but the door was locked. He looked quickly up and down the landing, and tapped quietly on the door. The sound seemed very loud on the silence. There was a long pause, and then he heard a key turning in the lock. The door eased open, and Bowman darted into the room. The door shut quietly behind him.

Katherine clung desperately to Bowman, holding him so tightly he could hardly breathe. She burrowed her face into his neck, as though trying to hide from the events of the day. He murmured soothingly to her, and after a while she quietened and relaxed her grip a little. He smiled slightly.

"Glad to see me, Kath?"

She lifted her face to his and kissed him hungrily. "I was so afraid you wouldn't come to me tonight. I need you, Edward. I need you now more than ever."

"It's all right, Kath. I'm here now."

"But if we're caught together . . ."

"We won't be," said Edward quickly. "Not as long as we're careful."

Katherine finally let go of him, and sat down on the edge of the bed. "*Careful.* I hate that word. We're always having to be careful, having to think twice about everything we do, everything we say. How much longer, Edward? How much longer before we can be together openly? I want you, my love; I want you with me always, in my arms, in my bed!''

''We won't have to keep up the pretence much longer,'' said Edward. ''Just for a while, till things have quietened down. All we have to do is be patient for a little while. . . .''

''I'm sick of being patient!''

Edward gestured sharply at the wall. Katherine nodded reluctantly, and lowered her voice before speaking again. It wouldn't do to be overheard, and there was no telling how thin the walls were.

''Edward, did the Guards say anything to you about who they think killed William?''

''Not really, but they'd be fools if they didn't see us as the main suspects. There's always been some gossip about us, and we both stood to gain by his death. We could have killed him. . . .''

''In a way, perhaps we did.''

''What?'' Edward looked at her sharply. ''Katherine, you didn't . . .''

''William committed suicide,'' said Katherine. ''I . . . told him about us.''

''You did what?''

''I had to! I couldn't go on like this, living a lie. I told him I was still fond of him, and always would be, but that I loved you and wanted to marry you. I said I'd do it any way he wanted, any way that would protect his political career, but that whatever happened I was determined on a divorce. To begin with he refused to listen, and then . . . then he told me he loved me, and would never give me up. I said I'd walk out on him if I had to, and he said that if I did, he would kill himself.''

"Dear God . . ." breathed Bowman. "And you think William . . ."

"Yes," said Katherine. "I think he killed himself. I think he died because of us."

"Have you told anyone else about this?"

"Of course not! But that's not all, Edward, I . . ."

She broke off suddenly and looked at the door. Out on the landing someone was walking past the door. Katherine rose quickly to her feet and held Edward's arm. They both stood very still, listening. The sound came again—soft, hesitant footsteps that died quickly away as they retreated down the landing. Bowman frowned. There was something strange about the footsteps. . . . Katherine started to say something, and Bowman hushed her with a finger to his lips. They listened carefully for a while, but the footsteps seemed to be gone.

"Did anyone see you come in here?" said Katherine quietly.

"I don't think so," said Bowman. "I was very careful. It could have been one of the Guards, just doing the rounds to make sure everything's secure. It could have been someone going to the bathroom. Whoever it was, they're gone now. I'd better get back to my room."

"Edward . . ."

"I can't stay, Kath. Not tonight, not here. It's too much of a risk. I'll see you again, in the morning."

"Yes. In the morning." Katherine kissed him goodbye, and then moved away to ease the door open a crack. The landing was completely deserted. Katherine opened the door wide, and Bowman slipped silently out onto the landing. She shut the door quietly behind him, and Bowman waited a moment while his eyes adjusted to the dimmer light. He started along the landing towards his own room, and then stopped as he heard a faint scuffing sound behind

him. He spun round, but there was no one there. The
landing stretched away before him, open and empty, until
it disappeared in the shadows at the top of the stairs. And
then the smell came to him—a sharp, musky smell that
raised the hackles on the back of his neck. Bowman reached
into the top of his boot and drew out a long slender dagger. The cool metal hilt felt good in his hand. He was in
danger; he could feel it. Bowman smiled grimly. If all this
was supposed to frighten him, his enemy was in for an
unpleasant surprise. He'd never backed away from a duel
in his life, and he'd never lost one. He wondered if this
was William's killer after all. He hoped so; he would enjoy
avenging William's death. He might not always have liked
the man, but he'd always admired him. Bowman stepped
forward, dagger in hand, and something awful came flying
out of the shadows at the top of the stairs. Bowman had
time to scream once, and then there was only the pain and
the blood, and the snarls of his attacker.

Hawk sat bolt upright in his chair as a scream rang out on
the landing and then was cut suddenly short. He jumped
to his feet, grabbed his axe and ran out of the parlour,
followed closely by Fisher with her sword in her hand. They
ran down the hall and pounded up the stairs together. The
first scream had been a man's scream, but now a woman
was screaming, on and on. Hawk drove himself harder,
taking the stairs two at a time. He burst out onto the landing and skidded to a halt as he looked around him for a
target.

   Edward Bowman lay twisted on the floor, his eyes wide
and staring. His clothes were splashed with blood, and
more had soaked into the carpet around him. His throat
had been torn out. Katherine Blackstone stood over the
body, screaming and screaming, her hands pressed to her

face in horror. Fisher took her by the shoulders and turned her gently away from the body. Katherine resisted at first, and then all the strength went out of her. She stopped screaming and stood in silence, her hands at her sides, staring blindly at the wall as tears ran unheeded down her cheeks. The other guests were spilling out of their doors in various stages of undress, all of them demanding to know what had happened. Hawk knelt beside the body. There was a dagger on the carpet, not far from Bowman's hand, but there was no blood on the blade. The attack must have happened so quickly that Bowman never even had a chance to defend himself. Hawk looked closely at Bowman's throat, and swore softly. The killer hadn't been as neat with Bowman as he had with Blackstone. Hawk sat back on his haunches and scowled thoughtfully at the body.

There were footsteps on the stairs behind him. He straightened up quickly and turned, axe in hand, to find Gaunt almost on top of him. He was wearing only a dressing gown, and looked flushed and out of breath.

"What is it?" he rasped, staring past Hawk. "What's happened?"

"Bowman's dead," said Hawk. "Murdered." He looked quickly around to see if anyone was missing, but all the guests were there, kept at a respectable distance from the body by Fisher's levelled sword. Dorimant was the nearest, with the witch Visage at his side. Their faces were white with shock. Lord and Lady Hightower stood in their doorway, halfway down the landing, both in their nightclothes. Lord Roderik was holding his wife protectively close to him. Stalker stood in the middle of the landing, his face set and grim, wearing only his trousers and boots but holding a sword in his hand. Hawk looked carefully at the sword, but there was no blood on the blade.

He looked again at Stalker, taking in the dozens of old scars that crisscrossed the huge muscular frame, and then looked away, wincing mentally.

"All right," said Hawk harshly. "Everyone downstairs. I can't work with all of you cluttering up the place. Stay in a group, and don't go off on your own for any reason. Don't argue, just move! You can wait in the parlour. You'll be all right; there's safety in numbers. Gaunt, you stay behind a minute."

Hawk waited impatiently as the guests filed past him, keeping well clear of the body. Lord and Lady Hightower helped Katherine down the stairs. Her tears had stopped, but her face was blank and empty from shock. Hawk stopped Stalker as he passed.

"I'll have to take your sword, sir Stalker."

Stalker looked at Hawk steadily, and his eyes were very cold. Fisher stepped forward, and lifted her blade a fraction. Stalker looked at her, and smiled slightly. He turned back to Hawk and handed him his sword, hilt first.

"Of course, Captain Hawk. There are tests you'll want to run."

"Thank you, sir warrior," said Hawk, sliding the sword through his belt. "The sword will be returned to you as soon as possible."

"That's all right," said Stalker. "I have others."

He followed the other guests down the stairs and into the parlour. Hawk and Fisher looked at each other, and relaxed a little.

"For a minute there," said Hawk, "I wondered . . ."

"Yeah," said Fisher. "So did I."

Hawk turned to Gaunt, who was kneeling by the body. "Careful, sir sorcerer. We don't want to destroy any evidence, do we?"

Gaunt nodded, and rose to his feet. "His throat's been

torn out. There's no telling what the murder weapon was; the wound's a mess.''

''That can wait for the moment,'' said Hawk. ''Is your isolation spell still holding?''

''Yes. I'd have known immediately if it had been breached. There can't be any more doubt; the killer has to be one of us.''

''All right,'' said Hawk. ''Go on down and wait with the others. And you'd better take a look at Katherine Blackstone. She's in shock. And coming so soon after the last shock to her system . . .''

''Of course,'' said Gaunt. He nodded quickly to Hawk and Fisher, then made his way back down the stairs. Hawk and Fisher looked thoughtfully at the body.

''We can't afford to wait till the experts get here in the morning,'' said Fisher. ''We've got to find the killer ourselves.''

''Right,'' said Hawk. ''If we don't, there might not be anybody left come the morning.''

5

Blood in the Night

"Well, first things first," said Hawk. "Let's check the body."

He and Fisher put away their weapons, knelt down beside Bowman, and studied the dead man carefully. Bowman's throat had been torn apart. Hawk frowned grimly as he examined the wounds.

"This wasn't done with a sword," he said slowly. "The edges of the wounds are ragged and uneven. It could have been a knife with a jagged edge. . . . See how it's ripped through the skin? What a mess. If I didn't know better, I'd swear Bowman had been attacked by some kind of animal."

"Right," said Fisher. "Take a look at his chest and arms."

There were long bloody rents in Bowman's shirtfront. Similar cuts showed on both his forearms, as though he'd held them up to try and protect his throat.

"Strange, that," said Hawk, indicating the torn and bloody arms. "If he had time to raise his arms, he should have had time to use his dagger. But there isn't a drop of blood on the blade.''

"Maybe he dropped it in the struggle," said Fisher. "It must have all happened pretty fast. Bowman never stood a chance. Poor bastard." She sank back on her haunches and stared unhappily at the body. "You know, Hawk, I wouldn't feel so bad if I hadn't disliked Bowman so much. There were times when I could quite happily have run the arrogant bastard through myself. I was so sure he was the murderer. . . ."

"I know what you mean," said Hawk. "I'd almost convinced myself he was the killer. It all made sense. He had both the motive and the opportunity . . . and I didn't like him either." He shook his head tiredly. "Well, we can't apologize to him now, lass. But maybe we can bring his killer to justice. So, with Bowman gone, who's the main suspect now?"

Fisher rubbed her jaw thoughtfully. "Katherine? She was first on the scene at both the murders."

"I don't think so," said Hawk. "A knife in the chest is one thing, but this . . . Whatever actually made these wounds, there must have been a hell of a lot of strength behind it to have done so much damage in so short a time. A starving wolf couldn't have done a better job on his throat. And remember, Katherine was standing right over the body when we found them, and there wasn't a trace of blood on her clothing."

"Very observant," said Fisher approvingly. "Whoever killed Bowman had to have got blood all over him. Did you see . . ."

"No," said Hawk. "I checked them all carefully as they filed past me, and no one had any blood on their clothes. The killer must have had time to change."

"Damn," said Fisher. "It would have simplified things."

"There's nothing simple about this case," said Hawk dourly. "We'd better check all the rooms, just in case there's some bloodstained clothing to be found, but I'm betting we won't find a damned thing. Our killer's too clever for that."

"What about Stalker's sword?" said Fisher suddenly.

"All right," said Hawk. "What about it?"

Fisher gave him a hard look. "You said you wanted to run some tests on it. What did you have in mind?"

"Nothing, really," said Hawk. "I just didn't want him looming over me with a sword in his hand. Remember, at the time all he had on were his trousers and boots. Where was his shirt? It occurred to me that he might have had to take it off because he'd got blood on it."

"I see," said Fisher. "You know, Hawk, we've been on some messy cases before, but this has got to be one of the messiest. Nothing makes sense. I mean, I can understand someone wanting Blackstone dead; he had more enemies than most of us make in a lifetime. But why Bowman? And why rip him apart like this?"

"Beats me," said Hawk. He got to his feet, and then bent down again to retrieve Bowman's dagger. He studied it a moment, and then tucked it into the top of his boot. Fisher got to her feet and looked about her. Hawk didn't miss that her hand was resting on the pommel of her sword. He looked down at Bowman's body. "Maybe . . ."

"Yeah?"

"Maybe he was just in the wrong place at the wrong time. He came out onto the landing, maybe to use the bathroom, and saw something or someone he shouldn't have. So the killer hit him then and there, on the spot. No time to be subtle or clever; just do the job."

Fisher thought about it. "That doesn't explain the savagery of the attack. Or the nature of the wounds. I don't know about the throat, but those cuts on his chest and arms look a hell of a lot like claw marks to me."

"So what does that mean? He was killed by an animal?"

"Not necessarily. Remember the Valley killer a couple of years back? Everyone thought it was a bear, and it turned out to be a man using a stuffed bear paw strapped to a club."

"Yeah," said Hawk. "I remember that case. But why should the killer use something weird like that, when a knife was good enough for Blackstone? Unless . . ."

"Unless what?" said Fisher as Hawk hesitated.

"Unless this is a different killer," said Hawk slowly. "Remember, Visage swore she'd kill Bowman in revenge for his murdering Blackstone. . . ."

"Two killers under one roof?" said Fisher incredulously. "Oh, come on, Hawk! It's hardly likely, is it? I know what the witch said, but that was just anger and grief talking. I mean, you saw her. Can you honestly see a timid, mousy little thing like her tearing into a man like this?"

"No, I suppose not." Hawk scowled suddenly. "Mind you, I have seen something like this before. . . ."

"Really? Where?"

"In the Hook," said Hawk grimly. He looked at the body, and shook his head angrily. "This case gets more complicated all the time. Come on, let's check the bedrooms. Maybe we'll get lucky."

"That'll be a change," said Fisher.

They started with the first door on the left at the top of the stairs, the spare room that Gaunt had opened up for Katherine after her husband's death. The room looked dusty and empty. The single oil lamp was still burning, and the bed obviously hadn't been slept in. The sheets hadn't even been turned back.

"Odd, that," said Hawk, looking at the bed. "She'd had a terrible shock, and Gaunt had given her a sedative, but she didn't go to bed. She should have been out on her feet, but she hadn't even changed into her nightclothes."

"Maybe she was waiting for someone," said Fisher. "Bowman, for example."

"Yeah," said Hawk. "That would explain what he was doing out on the landing. . . . Okay, let's take a look around."

"Apart from bloodstained clothing, what are we looking for?"

"Anything, everything. We'll know it when we see it."

"That's a great help, Hawk."

"You're welcome."

They searched the room slowly and methodically. It didn't take long. The wardrobe was empty, and so were most of the drawers in the dressing table. There wasn't anywhere else to hide anything. Hawk looked under the bed, just on general principles, but all he found were a few piles of fluff and an ancient chamber pot with a crack in it. He straightened up and looked vaguely about him, hoping for inspiration. Fisher was leaning over the dressing table.

"Found something, lass?"

"I'm not sure. Maybe. Come and take a look."

Hawk moved over to join her. Fisher had found a small wooden box pushed to the back of one of the dressing table's drawers. The wood had been nicely stained and polished, but there was nothing special about it. Hawk looked at Fisher enquiringly. She grinned, and flipped open the lid. A tangled mess of rings, earrings, and necklaces glistened brightly in the lamplight. There were gold and silver, emeralds and rubies and diamonds, all mixed carelessly together.

Hawk picked out a ring and inspected it closely. "Good quality," he said approvingly. He dropped the ring back into the jewel box, and studied the collection thoughtfully. "That little lot is probably worth more than both our annual salaries put together. And she didn't even bother to lock the case."

"Which means," said Fisher steadily, "that either she's very careless or she's got a lot more like that at home."

"Wouldn't surprise me," said Hawk. "So, what's your point?"

"Think about it, Hawk. Suppose Katherine and Bowman got together and decided to kill Blackstone, for the reasons we've already established. Then Katherine decides that while she still wants the prestige and the money, she doesn't need Bowman anymore. He comes to her room, they argue, there's a fight, and she kills him."

"With what?" said Hawk. "Where's the murder weapon? She was standing right over the body when we got there, so she couldn't have had much time to hide anything. And even though she was fully dressed, there wasn't a spot of blood on her. And anyway, we've got the same problem with her as we had with Visage. How could she possibly have caused wounds like those? Even if she had such a weapon, she's not exactly muscular, is she?"

"You'd be surprised what people can do, when they're angry enough," said Fisher darkly.

"Yeah, maybe. Let's try the next room."

The next room proved to be the bathroom. Hawk and Fisher stared open-mouthed at the gleaming tilework and the huge porcelain tub. It was at least six feet long and almost three feet wide. Beyond the tub was a delicate porcelain washstand with its own mirror, and a wonderfully crafted wooden commode.

"Now that's what I call luxury," said Fisher, bending over the bath and running her fingers lovingly over the smooth finish. "No more copper tub in front of the fire for me, Hawk. I want one of these."

"You have got to be joking," said Hawk. "Do you have any idea how much something like that costs? Besides, from what I've heard, those things aren't really healthy."

"Not healthy? How can a bath be not healthy?"

"Well, think of all the steam and water in such an enclosed space. You could end up with rheumatism."

"Oh, but think of the luxury," said Fisher wistfully. "Feel how smooth this is, Hawk. And imagine being able to stretch out in one of these, up to your chin in hot water, soaking for as long as you wanted. . . ." She looked at him sideways. "There might even be room for both of us. . . ."

"I'll order one tomorrow," said Hawk. "But you can ask for the raise we'll need in order to pay for it."

They chuckled quietly together, and then set about searching the bathroom. It didn't take long; there was nowhere to hide anything.

"I don't know," said Hawk finally. "Could something have been stuffed down the commode, do you think?"

"I wouldn't have thought so," said Fisher. "If it was blocked, it would probably have flooded over by now. Of course, there's only one way to be sure. . . ."

"If you think I'm sticking my hand down that thing, you're crazy," said Hawk. "It was just an idea, anyway. . . . Come on, let's try the next room."

"That's where we left Blackstone."

"We'd better take a quick look, just to be sure."

"What about Bowman?" said Fisher suddenly.

Hawk looked at her. "What about him?"

"Well, we can't just leave him lying out there on the landing, can we? I thought maybe we could put him in with Blackstone. At least he'd be out of the way there."

"Makes sense," said Hawk. "All right, let's move him."

They left the bathroom, and went back to where Bowman lay huddled on the landing. He looked smaller somehow, now that he was dead. Hawk took his shoulders while Fisher took the legs, and between them they got him off the floor. The carpet clung to Bowman's back for a moment, stuck there by the drying blood, and then he came free.

"He's heavier than he looks," said Fisher, panting a little as she backed away towards Blackstone's door.

"You should worry," said Hawk. "You've got the lighter end, if anything. And he's staring at me."

Fisher backed into the closed door and kicked it open. She and Hawk then manoeuvred Bowman's body through the doorway and dropped him unceremoniously on the floor next to Blackstone. They waited a moment while they got their breath back, and then looked about them. Hawk took in the uneven trail of blood Bowman's body had left behind on the landing carpet. He winced slightly. Gaunt wasn't going to be pleased.

Tough, thought Hawk. *I've got my own problems.*

"Doesn't look like anything's been moved," said Fisher.

"Yeah, but we'd better check anyway," said Hawk. "It shouldn't take long."

They checked the wardrobe and the dressing-table drawers and under the bed, and drew a blank every time. No trace of a murder weapon, or any bloodstained clothing.

"It was worth a try," said Hawk as he and Fisher stepped out onto the landing again.

"Yeah," said Fisher, pulling the door to behind her. "We're not doing very well, though, are we?"

"Not very," said Hawk. "But then, this isn't really our normal line of business. Locked-room murder mysteries are usually reserved for the experts. But . . ."

"Yeah," said Fisher. "*But*. We have to cope because we're all there is. Who does the next room belong to?"

"Bowman," said Hawk.

The room was clean and tidy, and the bed hadn't been slept in. Bowman's sword was still in its scabbard, hanging from the bedpost. Hawk drew the sword, checked the blade was clean, and then tried the balance. He nodded slowly. It was a good blade, long and thin and light.

"Duelling sword," said Fisher. "Apparently Bowman had something of a reputation as a duellist."

"Didn't help him at the end," said Hawk. "In fact, come to think of it, why wasn't he wearing his sword? After all, he was trapped in a strange house with a murderer on the loose. . . ."

"Yeah, but you don't wear a sword on a lover's tryst, do you?"

"If that was where he was going."

"Seems likely. Doesn't it?"

Hawk shrugged. "I suppose so." He sheathed Bowman's sword and dropped it onto the bed. He and Fisher moved quickly round the room, checking in all the usual places, and once again ended up with nothing to show for their pains.

"This is a waste of time," said Fisher. "We're never going to find anything."

"Probably not, but we have to check. How would it

seem if we missed some important piece of evidence, just because we couldn't be bothered to look for it?''

"Yeah, I know. Where next?''

"Across the hall,'' said Hawk. "Stalker's room.''

Fisher looked at him uncomfortably. "Are you serious about this, Hawk? I mean, can we really treat *Adam Stalker* as a suspect? He's a hero, a genuine hero. One of the greatest men this city ever produced. They were making up songs and legends about his exploits when I was still a child.''

"I don't trust songs or legends,'' said Hawk. "We check his room.''

"Why? Just because he wasn't wearing a shirt?''

"Partly. And also because he was one of the last people to arrive on the scene.''

Stalker's room looked lived in. His clothes lay scattered across the floor, as though he'd just dropped them wherever he happened to have taken them off. A broadsword in a battered leather scabbard lay across the foot of the bed. Hawk picked it up, and grunted in surprise at the weight of it. He drew the sword out, with some difficulty, and checked the blade. It was clean. Hawk took a firm grip on the hilt and hefted the sword awkwardly.

"How he swings this, even with both hands, is beyond me,'' he said finally.

"It probably helps if you're built like a brick out-house,'' said Fisher.

"Probably.'' Hawk slipped the sword back into its scabbard and dropped it onto the bed. He took a long look at the rumpled bed with its thrown-back sheets, and smiled sourly. "At least someone got some sleep tonight.''

"The joys of an undisturbed conscience,'' said Fisher, rummaging through the dressing-table drawers.

"Found anything?'' said Hawk.

"No. You?"

"No. I'm beginning to think I wouldn't recognise a clue if it walked up to me and pissed up my leg."

They checked all the usual places; no murder weapon, no bloodstained clothes.

"Let's try the next room," said Hawk. "That's Dorimant's, isn't it?"

"Yeah."

The room was neat and tidy, and the bed hadn't been slept in. They looked everywhere and found nothing.

"I could do this in my sleep," said Fisher disgustedly. "And if I was just a little more tired, I would."

"Only two more rooms, and we can call it a day," said Hawk.

"You mean a night."

"Whatever. The next room is the Hightowers'."

"Good. Let's make a mess."

Hawk chuckled. "You're getting vindictive, you."

"What do you mean, getting?"

The Hightowers' room was neat and tidy, and the bed had been slept in. Hawk and Fisher turned the place upside down, and didn't find anything. They conscientiously cleared up the mess they'd made, and moved on to the last room, feeling pleasantly virtuous. They felt even better when the usual search turned up a small wooden casket tucked under Visage's pillow. Hawk removed the casket carefully and placed it in the middle of the rumpled bed. It was about a foot square, and four inches deep, made from a dark yellow wood neither of them recognised. The lid was carved with enigmatic runes and glyphs that spilled over the edges and down the sides. Hawk reached out to open it, and Fisher grabbed his arm.

"I wouldn't. If that is a witch's casket, it could be booby-trapped with all kinds of spells."

Hawk nodded soberly. Fisher drew a dagger from the top of her boot, and cautiously slipped the tip of the blade into the narrow crack between the casket and its lid. She took a deep breath, flipped the lid open, and stepped quickly back. Nothing happened. Hawk and Fisher moved forward to look inside the casket. There were half a dozen bone amulets, two locks of dark hair, each tied with a green ribbon, and a few bundles of what appeared to be dried herbs. Fisher picked up one of the bundles and sniffed at it gingerly. It smelled a little like new-mown hay. Fisher dropped it back into the casket.

"You recognise any of this?" she asked quietly.

Hawk nodded slowly. "Those amulets are similar to the one Blackstone was wearing. I think we could be on to something here, Isobel. What if these are real protective amulets, and the one Blackstone was wearing was a fake? That way, everyone would think Blackstone was protected against magic, when actually he wasn't."

"If he could be attacked by magic," said Fisher patiently, "why bother to stab him? Besides, we know the amulet was magical. Gaunt detected it, remember?"

"Oh. Yeah. Damn."

He closed the casket, and put it back under the pillow again. He and Fisher took one last look round the room, and then went back out onto the landing, shutting the door behind them. They stood together a while, thinking.

"Well," said Hawk, "that was pretty much a waste of time."

"I told you that," said Fisher.

"It just doesn't make sense," said Hawk doggedly. "How could someone kill two men in a matter of hours, and then disappear without a trace?"

"Beats me," said Fisher. "Maybe there's an old secret passage, or something."

They looked at each other sharply.

"Now that is an idea," said Hawk. "A secret passage would explain a lot of things. . . . I think we'd better have a word with Gaunt."

"Worth a try," said Fisher, "but if he knew of any, he'd have told us by now. Unless he's the murderer, in which case he'd only lie anyway."

"This is true," said Hawk. "Let's check Blackstone's room anyway, just for the hell of it."

Fisher groaned wearily, and followed him down the hall and back into Blackstone's room. They moved slowly round the walls, tapping every foot or so and listening for a hollow sound. They didn't find one. They tried the floor, in case there was a trapdoor, and even had a good look at the ceiling, but to no avail. They stood together by the door and glared about them. Hawk shook his head irritably.

"If there is a secret passage here, it must be bloody well hidden."

"Secret passages usually are," said Fisher dryly. "If they weren't, they wouldn't be secret, would they?"

"You're so sharp you'll cut yourself one of these days," said Hawk. He took one last look round the room, and then frowned suddenly. "Wait a minute. . . . Something's wrong."

Fisher looked round the room, but couldn't see anything out of place. "What do you mean, wrong?"

"I don't know. Something here isn't quite the way I remember it." He glared about him, trying to work out what had changed. And then he looked down at Blackstone's body, and the answer came to him. "The wineglass! It's gone!"

He got down on his knees beside Blackstone's body. The wine stain on the carpet was still there, but the glass

Blackstone had been drinking from was gone. Hawk peered under the bed in case the glass had rolled away, but there was no sign of it.

"Was it there the first time we checked this room?" asked Fisher.

"I don't know. I didn't look. Did you see it?"

"No. I didn't look either. I wouldn't have noticed it was gone now if you hadn't spotted it."

Hawk straightened up slowly. "Well, at least that tells us something."

"Like what?" said Fisher.

"It tells us the wineglass was important," said Hawk. "If it wasn't, why bother to remove it? In some way, that wineglass must have played an important part in Blackstone's death."

"The wine wasn't poisoned," said Fisher. "Gaunt told us that."

"Yeah," said Hawk. "He also said he was going to take a sample of the wine so that he could run some tests on it. We'd better check that he did."

"If he didn't, we're in bother."

"Right." Hawk scowled fiercely. "Why should the wine be important? I'm missing something, Isobel, I can feel it. It's important, and I'm missing it."

Fisher waited patiently as Hawk concentrated, trying to grasp the elusive thought, but in the end he just shook his head.

"No. Whatever it is, I can't see it. Not yet, anyway. Let's go downstairs. I want to check the lower rooms as well, before I talk to Gaunt about the wine sample."

"And if he didn't take one?"

"Burn that bridge when we come to it." Hawk looked down at the two bodies lying side by side on the floor.

"I've got a bad feeling about this, Isobel. I don't think our murderer is finished with us yet."

Hawk thought furiously as he and Fisher made their way down the stairs and into the hall. He'd gone about as far as he could on his own. If he was going to get any further, he had to have more information from Gaunt and his guests, and that meant more cooperation on their part. Some would cooperate, some might, and some wouldn't. In theory, he could order them to do anything and they were legally obliged to obey him, but in reality he had to be very careful about what orders he gave. Most of his suspects were important people in Haven. They had a great deal of clout, if they chose to use it. Hawk worried his lower lip between his teeth. If and when he felt able to accuse someone, he'd better have overwhelming evidence to back him up. Nothing else would do.

Unfortunately, evidence was in very short supply at the moment. All he had were endless theories, none of which seemed to lead anywhere. He couldn't be sure of anything anymore. He stopped suddenly at the foot of the stairs, and looked down the hall at the closed front door. Fisher stopped beside him and looked at him curiously.

"Hawk, what is it?"

"I just had an intriguing thought," said Hawk. "We've been assuming that no one could get in or out of this house because of the isolation spell. Right?"

"Right."

"How do we know there is an isolation spell?"

"Gaunt said so. And besides, we felt the effects when he cast it."

Hawk shook his head. "Gaunt has said a lot of things. We felt a spell being cast, all right, but how do we know it was an isolation spell? Could have been anything. You go into the parlour and talk to Gaunt a minute. Keep him occupied. I'm going to open that front door and see if we really are isolated from the outside world.''

Fisher nodded reluctantly. ''All right. But you be careful, Hawk.''

Hawk grinned, and set off down the hall as Fisher went into the parlour. The hall was large and gloomy, and the shadows seemed very dark. His footsteps echoed loudly on the quiet. He finally came to a halt before the closed front door, and looked it over carefully. It looked normal enough. He reached out his left hand and gently pressed his fingers to the wood. It felt strangely cold to the touch, and seemed almost to pulse under his fingertips. Hawk snatched his hand away and rubbed his fingers together. They were still cold. Hawk braced himself, and took a firm hold of the door handle. It seemed to stir in his hand, and he tightened his grip. He turned the handle all the way round, and then eased the door open a crack. The hall was suddenly very cold. Hawk opened the door a little wider and looked out. And outside the door there was nothing; nothing at all.

Hawk clung desperately to the door. It was like standing on a narrow ledge and looking out over a bottomless drop. No matter where he looked there was only the dark, as though the house were falling on and on into an endless night. A cold wind blew from nowhere, searing his bare face and hands. Hawk swallowed sickly, and with a great effort tore his eyes away from the dark. He stepped back, and slammed the door shut. He moved quickly away from the door and leaned against the nearest wall while he got his breath back. His hands and face were numb from the cold, but feeling quickly returned as the summer heat inside the house drove the cold out of him. He smiled slightly. If nothing else, he had established that the house was very definitely isolated from the outside world. He wondered how Fisher was getting on.

When Fisher had entered the parlour, the assembled guests met her with a frosty silence. They were sitting together in a group, having apparently discovered that there was comfort as well as safety in numbers. They made an ill-assorted group, with some fully dressed and some still in their nightclothes. Katherine Blackstone was once again sitting by the empty fireplace. She'd regained some of her composure, but her face was still very pale and her eyes were red and swollen. She held a handkerchief in one hand as though she'd forgotten it was there. Stalker sat beside her, drinking thirstily from a newly filled glass of wine. Lord and Lady Hightower sat together, staring into the empty fireplace, both lost in their own thoughts. Visage had pulled her chair up next to Dorimant's, and she leaned tiredly against him, his arm round her shoulders. The young witch looked frightened and confused, while Dorimant looked stubbornly protective. Gaunt was sitting nearest the door, and stood up as Fisher entered.

"Well, Captain Fisher, what have you found?"

"Nothing particularly helpful, sir sorcerer. Judging from the extent of his wounds, it seems likely Edward Bowman was attacked by a madman or an animal. Or by someone who wanted it to look like an animal attack."

Gaunt raised an eyebrow. "Why should anyone want to do that?"

"Beats me," said Fisher. "Nothing in this case seems to make sense."

"Some things never do, girl," said Stalker. "You learn that as you get older."

Fisher looked at him sharply. There had been something in his voice, something . . . bitter. Stalker finished off the last of his wine and stared moodily into the empty glass. Fisher turned back to Gaunt.

"Earlier on this evening, Hawk asked you to run some tests on the wine Blackstone was drinking just before his death," she said quietly. "Did you take a sample to test?"

"I'm afraid not," said Gaunt. "I was going to do it first thing in the morning."

"Damn."

"Is there a problem, Captain Fisher?"

"You could say that. Someone has removed the wine-glass from Blackstone's room."

"You should have put a guard on the door," said Lord Hightower suddenly. His voice was flat and harsh.

"We could have, my Lord," said Fisher. "But we thought it more important to protect all of you against further attacks."

"You failed at that too," said Hightower. "I'll have your heads for this incompetence, both of you!"

Fisher started to answer him, and then stopped as Gaunt's head suddenly snapped round to stare at the hall.

"Someone's trying to open the front door!"

"It's all right, sir Gaunt," said Fisher quickly. "It's only Hawk. He's just checking that the house is properly secure."

Gaunt relaxed a little, and stared sardonically at Fisher. "You mean he's checking the isolation spell. What's the matter, Captain? Don't you trust me anymore?"

"We don't trust anyone," said Fisher carefully. "That's our job, sir sorcerer."

Gaunt nodded curtly. "Of course, Captain. I understand."

"Then you'll also understand why we have to search all the rooms on the ground floor."

Gaunt frowned. "You've already seen them once."

"Not all of them, sir sorcerer. We haven't seen the kitchen, or your laboratory."

"My laboratory is strictly private," said Gaunt. "No one uses it but me. There's really no need for you to check it; you felt the avoidance spell yourself. It's impossible for anyone to enter the laboratory apart from myself."

"We'll still have to check it," said Fisher.

"I can't allow that," said Gaunt flatly.

"I'm afraid I must insist."

"No."

"Then we'll have to arrest you," said Fisher.

"On what charge?"

"We'll think of something."

Gaunt smiled coldly. "Do you really think you have the power to arrest me?" he said softly.

"We can give it a damn good try," said Hawk.

Everyone looked round to see Hawk standing in the parlour doorway, axe in hand. Gaunt started to raise his left hand, and then stopped as Fisher drew her sword in a single swift movement that set the tip of her blade against his ribs. Gaunt stood very still. The guests watched in a fascinated silence. Hawk took a firm grip on his axe. The tension in the parlour stretched almost to breaking point. And then Gaunt took a deep breath and let it out, and some of the strength seemed to go out of him with it.

"I could kill you both," he said quietly, "but what would be the point? They'd only send somebody else. And much as it pains me to admit it, you're the best chance I've got of finding William's killer. I will show you my laboratory. But if either of you ever draws steel on me again, I'll strike you down where you stand. Is that clear?"

"I hear you," said Hawk. "Now let's take a look at this laboratory of yours. Fisher, you come with us. Everyone else, stay here. We won't be long."

"One moment," said Stalker, rising unhurriedly to his feet. "You still have my sword, Captain Hawk. I'm afraid I must ask you to return it. With the murderer still loose in the house, somebody has to be able to protect these people."

Hawk nodded reluctantly, drew Stalker's sword from his belt, and stepped forward to hold it out to Stalker hilt first. Although it was nowhere near as heavy as Stalker's broadsword, the weight of the sword was still almost too much for Hawk to support one-handed. Stalker took the sword from him as though it were a child's toy. Hawk bowed politely, and turned to Gaunt.

"Shall we go, sir sorcerer?"

Gaunt led the way out of the parlour, across the hall, and into the library in tight-lipped silence. Hawk and Fisher followed close behind. Neither of them had put away their weapons. Gaunt opened the door into the kitchen and waved Hawk and Fisher through. They had a quick look round, but it looked like any other well-stocked kitchen, though surprisingly tidy for a man living on his own. They went back into the library, and found Gaunt standing before the laboratory door.

"Your partner asked me about the wine sample," said Gaunt, not looking around. "I'm afraid I didn't take one. But I can assure you the wine was perfectly harmless. My magic would have told me if it was poisonous. I even tasted some myself, remember?"

"That's not really the point," said Hawk patiently. "The wineglass must have been important in some way, or it wouldn't have been taken. Did Fisher ask you about the secret passages?"

"No," said Gaunt. "I can see what you're suggesting, Captain, but there are no secret passages or hidden doors in this house. If there were, my magic would have found them.''

"I see," said Hawk. "Well, then, I think that's all we have to talk about, sir sorcerer. Now, why don't you take off the avoidance spell and open that door?''

"I can't," said Gaunt quietly. "There is no avoidance spell.''

Hawk and Fisher looked at each other, and then at the sorcerer.

"Then what the hell was it we felt?'' asked Hawk.

Gaunt turned round and looked at them. He held his head high but his eyes were full of a quiet desperation. "She is my Lady," he said simply. "No one knows she's here. No one but me, and now you. If either of you ever talk about her to anyone else, I'll kill you. You'll understand why when you see her.''

He turned back to the door and took a key from a hidden inner pocket. Hawk and Fisher looked at each other and shrugged. Gaunt unlocked the door, pushed it open, and walked forward into his laboratory. Hawk and Fisher followed him in, and then stopped just inside the doorway. Hawk clutched at his axe, and Fisher lifted her sword. The succubus smiled at them sweetly.

She reclined lazily in the pentacle, her feet just brushing the edge of the blue chalk lines. Hawk swallowed dryly. He'd never seen anyone so beautiful. He wanted her, he had to have her; he'd kill anyone who tried to stop him. He stepped forward, and Fisher grabbed his arm. He tried to pull free, and when he couldn't he spun furiously on Fisher and lifted his axe to split her skull. Their eyes met, and he hesitated. Reality came flooding back, and he slowly lowered his axe, horrified at what he'd almost done. He looked at the succubus again, and felt the same insane desire stir within him. He fought it down ruthlessly, and wouldn't look away until he was sure the beautiful creature no longer had any hold over him. He looked at Gaunt, standing beside him with his head bowed.

"You fool," said Hawk softly. "You bloody fool."

"Yes," said Gaunt. "Oh, yes."

The succubus laughed sweetly. "Visitors. It's not often I'm allowed visitors."

Fisher stirred uncomfortably. "Is that what I think it is?"

"Yes," said Hawk grimly. "That's a succubus. A female demon, the embodiment of sexual attraction."

Fisher looked at the creature in the pentacle, and shuddered. She felt a strange attraction burning deep within her, and her skin crawled. She shook her head sharply, and the feeling slowly died away. Fisher glared coldly at Gaunt. "No wonder you didn't want us in here. Your friends in the parlour would disown you in a moment at the merest hint that you kept a succubus under your roof. When did you summon her out of the dark?"

"A long time ago," said Gaunt. "Please. She's no danger to anyone. She can't leave the pentacle except at my bidding, and she can't leave the house at all. My wards see to that."

"You let her out once, though, didn't you?" said Hawk. "You let her loose in the Hook, and she killed at your command."

"Yes," said Gaunt. "But that was the only time. She was under my control. . . ."

"I was there," said Hawk harshly. "I saw what she did to those men. It took weeks to get the stench of the blood off the streets. She's too dangerous, Gaunt. It would only take one slip on your part, and she'd be loose. With her power, she could destroy all Haven in a single night. You have to dismiss her, Gaunt. You have to send her back into the darkness."

"I can't," said Gaunt miserably. "Do you think I haven't tried? To begin with I couldn't because she was the source of my power. Without her, I was just another alchemist, with only a smattering of the High Magic. And then . . . I grew to need her. She's like a drug I have to have. Women don't mean anything to me anymore; they can't compare with her. I have to have her. I can't give her up. I won't. If you try to make me, I'll kill you."

His voice was uneven and feverish, and there was a fey look in his eyes. Fisher lifted her sword a little.

"Don't," said Hawk quickly. Fisher looked at him, and Hawk smiled grimly. "Unfortunately, if Gaunt dies his hold over the demon is gone, and she would be free of all restraints. For the time being at least, we have to keep him alive."

"Am I really so terrible?" asked the succubus. Her voice was slow and deep and soft as bitter honey. "I am love and joy and pleasure. . . ."

"And you'd kill us all if it weren't for that pentacle," said Hawk. "I've met demons before. You kill to live, and live to kill. You know nothing but destruction." He met her gaze unflinchingly with his one remaining eye, and the succubus looked away first.

"You're strong," said the succubus. "Such a pity. Still, I think I'll enjoy killing you, when the time comes. After all, Gaunt can't deny me anything. Can you, darling?"

"These death threats are starting to get on my nerves," said Fisher. "The next person to threaten Hawk or me is going to regret it, because I will personally chop them into chutney. You remember, demon: a sword blade doesn't care how powerful you are."

The succubus just smiled at her.

"Please," said Gaunt. "There's no need for any of this. As you can see, there's nowhere here an assassin could be hiding. You must leave. Now."

Hawk looked around him, refusing to be hurried. The laboratory was jammed with solid wooden benches, half-buried under various alchemical equipment, and all four walls were lined with simple wooden shelves bearing stoppered glass bottles in various sizes. Fisher moved over to examine some of the bottles. One large specimen contained a severed monkey's head. Fisher leaned forward to get a closer look, and the head opened its eyes and smiled at her. She stepped back, startled. The monkey's head winked at her slyly, and then closed its eyes again.

"Hawk," said Fisher, "let's get the hell out of here."

Hawk nodded, and he and Fisher backed slowly out of the laboratory and into the library. Neither of them felt entirely safe in turning their backs on the succubus. Gaunt backed out after them. The succubus blew him a kiss, and chuckled richly. Gaunt slammed the door shut on her, and locked it. When he turned round to face Hawk and Fisher, they saw a sheen of sweat on his face. He squared his shoulders and did his best to meet their accusing eyes.

"I know I have to get rid of her," he said quietly. "Perhaps when this is over . . ."

"Yes," said Hawk. "Perhaps. We'll talk more about this later. In the meantime, I want you to do something for me."

"If I can," said Gaunt. "What is it?"

"I want you to set up a truthspell."

The sorcerer frowned. "Are you sure that's wise, Captain?"

"You can do it, can't you?"

"Of course I can do it," snapped Gaunt. "It's not exactly a complicated spell; in fact, it's something of an interest of mine. But the spell only lasts for a limited time, and if you're not very careful about the questions you ask, the answers you get will be worthless. There are all kinds of truth, Captain Hawk. And I should point out that some of the people here aren't going to take kindly to the idea of being questioned under a truthspell. . . ."

"I'll deal with that," said Hawk. "All you have to do is set up the spell. I take full responsibility."

"Very well," said Gaunt. "Where do you want the spell cast?"

"In the parlour," said Hawk. "Why don't you go on in and break the news to them? They might take it better, coming from you. Fisher and I will join you in a minute."

Gaunt bowed politely and left the library. Hawk waited until the door was closed, and then sank tiredly into the nearest chair. Fisher pulled up another chair and sat down beside him.

"A succubus . . ." said Hawk slowly. "I'd heard about such things, but I never thought I'd actually meet one."

"Right," said Fisher. "I feel like I want to take a bath, just from being in the same room with her. All right, she was beautiful, but she made my skin creep every time she looked at me."

"Yeah," said Hawk.

They sat in silence a while, thinking.

"Hawk, do you really think Gaunt let the succubus loose in the Hook?"

"It seems likely."

"The bodies you found there; you said they'd been ripped apart. Like Bowman?"

Hawk frowned. "Not really; the Hook was much worse. But I see your point, Isobel. The succubus has to be a suspect, either as the murderer or the murder weapon. Gaunt can let her out of that pentacle any time he likes.

At the time of the first murder Gaunt said he was in the kitchen, but he could easily have slipped out long enough to release the succubus. All he had to do was go via the library, and we'd never have seen him. The succubus's powers are probably limited in the house by the sorcerer's wards, but she could still have killed Blackstone and Bowman while Gaunt remained in plain view, giving him a perfect alibi.''

"Except he wasn't in plain view during either of the murders," said Fisher. "Besides, could something like a succubus prowl around the house without Visage detecting it?"

"I don't know," said Hawk. "She sensed there was something nasty in the library, even though the demon was shielded by the pentacle. But then again, she's not in the same class as Gaunt. . . ."

"A succubus," said Fisher. "Just what we needed. Another suspect with magical powers."

Hawk laughed. "It's not that bad, lass. If the succubus had intended to kill someone, I really can't see her stabbing them neatly through the heart and then scurrying back later to steal their wineglass. It doesn't make sense."

"When has this case ever made sense?"

"You might just have a point there," said Hawk. "Come on, let's get back to the parlour. Maybe the truth-spell will help to sort things out."

"We're going to have some trouble there," said Fisher. "They're really not going to be happy about the truth-spell."

"I don't give a rat's arse," said Hawk. "One way or the other, I'm going to get some answers out of them, and to hell with the consequences."

Fisher looked at him fondly. "What the hell; we're still young. We can get other jobs. Let's do it."

They left the library and went into the parlour. The guests were arguing furiously with Gaunt. Hawk raised his voice and called for everyone's attention. There was a sudden hush as everyone turned to stare at him. He looked about him, taking in the silent, hostile faces, and knew that Gaunt hadn't been able to persuade them. Not that he'd expected it for one minute.

"Just in case there's any doubt among you," he said steadily, "Edward Bowman is dead. From the nature of his wounds, it's clear it was a frenzied and vicious attack. This second murder means that I have no choice but to proceed with the official investigation now, rather than wait for my superiors in the morning. I have therefore instructed the sorcerer Gaunt to set up a truthspell."

Instead of the babble of outrage he'd expected, Hawk found himself facing a stubborn, unyielding silence. They'd all clearly decided they weren't going to cooperate. *That's the trouble with politics,* thought Hawk sourly. *Everyone's got something to hide.*

"I'm sorry," he said firmly, "but I have to insist."

"You can insist all you like," said Lord Hightower flatly. "I won't answer any of your damned questions."

"The law is quite clear, my Lord. . . ."

"To hell with the law and to hell with you."

Hawk sighed quietly. "In that case, my Lord, we'll just have to do it the hard way. I will instruct the sorcerer Gaunt to prepare a truth drug. I will then knock you down, and Fisher will kneel on your chest while I feed you the drug."

Hightower's jaw dropped. "You wouldn't dare!"

"Oh, yes he would," said Fisher, moving forward to stand beside Hawk. "And so would I. One way or another, my Lord, you will answer our questions, just like everyone else. I'd advise you to settle for the truthspell. It's so much more dignified."

Hightower looked at Hawk and Fisher, and saw that they meant it. For a moment he considered defying them anyway, but the moment passed. He held his wife's hand tightly. There were ways round a truthspell. To start with, it couldn't compel him to talk.

Hawk took Hightower's silence for assent and looked round to see if there were any further objections. Lady Hightower was glaring daggers at him, and Stalker was frowning thoughtfully, but nobody had anything to say.

Gaunt stepped forward. "Everything is ready, Captain Hawk. We can begin whenever you wish."

"I'm not too clear on what a truthspell entails," said Dorimant hesitantly. "How does it work?"

"It's really very simple," said Gaunt. "Once the spell is cast, no one in this room will be able to tell a lie for a period of about twenty to twenty-five minutes. The duration of the spell is limited by the number of people involved. You can of course refuse to speak, or even evade the question, but that in itself tells us something. For as long as the spell lasts, nothing can be said but the absolute truth."

"If we're going to do some serious talking, how about a little wine to wet our whistles before we start?" said Stalker. He held up the bottle of white wine he'd been using to fill his own glass.

"Hold it," said Hawk. "I'm not too keen on wine at the moment. Gaunt, can you check it hasn't been tampered with?"

"Of course," said Gaunt. He gestured lightly with his left hand, and the wine seemed to stir briefly in the bottle. "It's perfectly sound, Captain. Not one of my better vintages, but . . ."

Stalker shrugged. "With your taste in wine, it's hard to tell. Now, who's for a drink?"

It seemed everybody was. Gaunt passed round the glasses, and Stalker poured the wine. People began to relax a little. Stalker left Hawk to last, and gestured with his head that he wanted to speak privately with him. They moved away a few feet.

"Just a thought," said Stalker quietly, "about the locked room. You staked a vampire earlier today, right?"

"Right," said Hawk. "What's that got to do with anything?"

"Think about it," said Stalker. "Vampires are shape-shifters, remember? They can turn themselves into bats, or even into mist."

Hawk nodded slowly. "Right . . . A locked door wouldn't stop a vampire, not once it had been invited into the house. It could turn to mist and seep through the cracks round the door! No, wait a minute; it doesn't work."

"Why not?"

"The undead don't usually need to stab their victims with a knife. And besides, vampires don't eat or drink; they can't. But everyone here was invited to dinner, and I've seen everybody with a glass in their hand at one stage or another. No, it's a nice idea, but there are too many ways a vampire would have given himself away by now. Thanks anyway, sir Stalker."

"You're welcome. It was just a thought." Stalker moved back to rejoin the others.

"If everyone would care to take a seat," said Gaunt, "we can begin."

Hawk and Fisher and the guests pulled up chairs in a rough semicircle facing the sorcerer. He waited patiently till they were settled, and then made a sweeping motion with his left hand. Time seemed to slow and stop. Gaunt spoke a single word of Power and there was a sudden jolt as the whole room shook. There was a vague tension in the air, and then everything snapped back to normal. Hawk frowned. He didn't feel any different.

"Who's going to ask the questions?" said Gaunt.

"I will," said Hawk. "I suppose we'd better start with a test. My partner is . . ." He tried to say the word *short*, and found he couldn't. His mouth simply wouldn't form the word. "Tall," he said finally. "Your spell seems to be working quite efficiently, sir sorcerer."

Gaunt nodded calmly. Fisher gave Hawk a hard look, and he smiled awkwardly. He looked quickly round the assembled guests, and braced himself. *All right; in at the deep end.*

"Sir Gaunt, let's start with you."

"Very well."

"You are a sorcerer."

"Yes."

"Did you kill Blackstone and Bowman?"

"No."

"Did you bring about their deaths indirectly, by use of your magic?"

"No."

"You have an acquaintance, who helped you in the Hook. Is that person in any way associated with the murders?"

"That is . . . highly unlikely."

He didn't say it was impossible, thought Hawk. *Let's push this a little further.*

"You were once sorcerer to the King," he said carefully.

"Yes."

"You quarrelled with him."

"Yes."

"Was it about your acquaintance?"

"In a way."

"What happened? Why did you leave the Court and come here, to Haven?"

Gaunt hesitated, and then sighed jerkily. "The King wanted her for himself, and I wouldn't give her up. I couldn't. So I came here, to . . . work things out on my own."

"Wait a minute," said Lord Hightower. "Who are you two talking about? What's this woman got to do with anything?"

"Apparently nothing," said Hawk. "Please relax, my Lord; we'll get to you in good time. That's all for the moment, sir sorcerer. Now then, sir Dorimant . . ."

"I didn't kill them," said Dorimant quickly.

"I have to ask the question," said Hawk politely. "Otherwise your answer won't mean anything. Did you kill Blackstone and Bowman?"

"No. No, I didn't."

Hawk looked at him narrowly. Dorimant was sitting awkwardly in his chair. His smile was weak and his eyes were evasive. *He's hiding something*, thought Hawk. *I wonder what?*

"You said earlier that Visage was with you at the time of the first murder," he said slowly. "Was that true?"

"Yes," said Dorimant, though he didn't look too happy about admitting it.

"Why was she with you?" said Hawk.

Dorimant looked at Visage, who bit her lip and then nodded unhappily. Dorimant looked back at Hawk. "She was the first one to find William's body," he said reluctantly. "She'd gone to his room to talk to him, and found him lying dead on the floor. She came to me for help."

Everyone sat up straight in their chairs. Hawk felt a

sudden rush of excitement as he finally put two and two together. He looked at Visage.

"The room wasn't locked when you found him? You just walked right in?"

"Yes," said Visage. "It wasn't locked."

"Of course," said Hawk happily. "That's it! That's what I've been missing all along!"

Fisher looked at him dubiously. "What are you going on about, Hawk?"

Hawk grinned. "I've finally worked out how the murder took place in a room locked from the inside. Simple: the door was never locked to begin with!"

"Of course the door was locked," said Fisher. "You had to break it down with your axe! I was there, remember?"

"How did you know the door was locked?" said Hawk. "Did you try to open it?"

"Well, no . . ."

"Exactly. Neither did I. Katherine came down and told us the door was locked. We went back with her, but she was careful to get to the door first. She rattled the door handle convincingly, told us again that it wouldn't open, and ordered me to break the door down. Afterwards, the lock was such a mess we couldn't tell it hadn't been locked. And that's why we found the key on the floor, and not in the lock."

Everyone looked at Katherine, who stared at the floor with her head bowed.

"Is this true?" asked Gaunt.

Katherine nodded tiredly. "Yes. I lied about the door being locked. But I didn't kill William."

"If you didn't, then who did?" said Stalker.

"No one," said Katherine, looking up for the first time. "He committed suicide."

"What?" said Fisher. "You have to got to be joking!"

Everyone started talking at once. Hawk yelled for quiet, and went on yelling till he got it. The voices died away to a rebellious silence as Hawk glared impartially about him.

"Let's take this from the beginning," he said grimly. "Visage, you found Blackstone's body. Tell us what happened."

Visage glanced briefly at Dorimant for support, and then began her story in a low whisper.

"I wanted to talk to William. There was something about Gaunt's house that made me feel uneasy, and I wanted to be sure he was wearing his amulet of protection."

"The one you designed for him," said Hawk.

"Yes. Stalker gave me the idea. He'd seen something like it in his travels."

Hawk looked at Stalker, who nodded. "That's right, Captain. They're very common in the East, and with all the recent threats I thought the amulet might be a good idea. I explained the theory to Visage, and she made the amulet for William."

"All right," said Hawk. "Go on, Visage."

"I went to William's room and knocked on the door. There was no answer, but the door was ajar, so I pushed it open. William was lying on the floor. I ran over to him and checked his breathing, but he was already dead."

"Did you touch the knife?" asked Fisher.

"There wasn't any knife," said Visage flatly. "When I found William, there wasn't a mark on him. I saw the wineglass by his hand, and I assumed one of his enemies had poisoned him. I didn't know what to do. I know I should have gone to you, Captain Hawk, but I was afraid to. I was the one who'd found him, and I thought I'd be blamed. . . . I panicked, that's all. I ran back to Graham's room and told him what I'd found. He was kind to me. He said that we'd go and tell you together, and say that we'd both found the body. We were just getting ready to go downstairs when we heard you breaking down William's door. And then . . . well, we heard about the knife and the locked door, and we didn't know what to think. Graham never doubted me, but . . . In the end, we decided to say nothing. I was afraid you wouldn't believe me, and I didn't want Graham to get into trouble by supporting me.''

Hawk waited a moment, but Visage said nothing more. He looked at Dorimant. ''Is this true? You conspired to conceal evidence in a murder case? Even though the victim was your friend?''

''I had to,'' said Dorimant. ''You and your partner have a reputation for violence. I had to protect Visage. William would have understood.''

''Let me just check that I've got this straight,'' said Fisher. ''Visage found Blackstone's body before Katherine did. Only then, the door wasn't locked and there was no knife wound. Katherine finds the body later, brings us up to see it, but fools us into thinking the door is locked when it isn't, and never was. And when we find the body, there's a knife in Blackstone's chest.'' Fisher looked at Katherine. ''I think you've got some explaining to do.''

Katherine Blackstone looked at the glass of wine in her hand. She hadn't drunk any. ''Captain Hawk was right about the locked door,'' she said finally, ''But I had to do it. When we first left the parlour and went upstairs to change for dinner, I went to visit Edward Bowman in his room. We were lovers. When I returned to my own room, I pushed the door open to find my husband lying dead on the floor, a half-empty wineglass lying by his hand. Like Visage, I thought immediately of poison, but I knew it wasn't murder. It was suicide. A few days ago I finally confessed to William about my love for Edward. I was going to divorce my husband, in order to marry Edward. William threatened to kill himself if I left him.'' She looked pleadingly at Hawk and Fisher. ''Don't you understand? I *couldn't* let his death be suicide! The scandal would have destroyed his reputation, and everything he'd achieved. People believed in William; he was Reform. The truth about me and William and Edward would have been bound to come out, and William's enemies would have used the scandal to undo everything he'd achieved. My life would have been ruined, and Edward's political career would have been at an end. I had to protect my husband's reputation, for all our sakes. So I took William's knife from his boot and thrust it into his chest, to make it look like a murder. As a martyr, William could still serve the party he founded. Particularly, if no murderer was ever found. And how could the killer be found, when there never was any murder?''

There was a long pause. Hightower stirred restlessly.

''That is possibly the most ludicrous story I have ever heard,'' he said finally.

''But true,'' said Gaunt. ''Every word of it. The truth-spell is still in force.''

''So William killed himself,'' said Dorimant.

''I don't think so,'' said Hawk. ''I can see how it would have looked that way to you, Katherine, but I still believe your husband was murdered. You see, the wineglass has mysteriously disappeared from Blackstone's room.''

''The wine wasn't poisoned,'' said Gaunt. ''I checked. I even tasted it myself.''

''It still has to be significant,'' said Hawk stubbornly, ''or it wouldn't have been taken. But we can come back to that later. Katherine, is there anything else about your husband's death that you haven't told us? Anything else that you've concealed from us?''

''No. There's nothing else. I didn't kill my husband, and I didn't kill Edward.''

Hawk thought a moment, and then turned to look at Visage. ''Did you kill Blackstone and Bowman?''

''No,'' said the witch quietly. ''William was already dead when I found him. And I don't know anything about what happened to Edward. Although . . .''

''Yes?'' said Hawk.

Visage frowned. ''There was a funny smell on the landing. . . .''

Hawk waited, but she said nothing more. He turned to face Lord Hightower. ''My Lord . . .''

''I object to this whole proceeding.''

''Just answer the questions, my Lord. Did you kill Blackstone and Bowman?''

''No,'' said Lord Roderik. ''I did not.''

Hawk looked at him thoughtfully. He couldn't think of any more specific questions to ask the Lord Hightower, and he had a strong feeling that what answers he did get would be as unhelpful as Hightower could make them. Hawk sighed silently. He could tell Lord Hightower was edgy about something—it was plain in his face and his manner—but there was nothing he could do about it for the moment. If he did put the pressure on, and found nothing to justify his actions . . . Hawk turned to the Lady Hightower.

''My Lady, did you kill Blackstone and Bowman?''

''No.''

Hawk looked at her for a moment, but her level eyes and the tight line of her mouth made it clear that he wasn't going to get anywhere with her either. Hawk scowled. The truthspell had seemed like such a good idea at the time. . . . He turned to Stalker.

"Sir Stalker, did you kill Blackstone and Bowman?"

"No."

Hawk sat back in his chair and frowned thoughtfully. He'd asked everybody outright, and each had denied being the murderer. That was impossible. One of them had to be the killer, so one of them must be lying. But since the truthspell was still in force, they couldn't be lying. . . . He thought hard. He was missing something again; he could feel it.

"Sir Stalker . . ."

"Yes, Captain Hawk."

"Whoever the killer is, he must have extensive knowledge of this house, to be able to move about it as freely as he has. Gaunt told me earlier that you had been very insistent in your attempts to buy this house. Perhaps you could tell me why this house is so important to you."

Stalker hesitated. "I can assure you my reasons have nothing to do with killing Blackstone and Bowman."

"Please answer the question, sir Stalker."

"This used to be my home," said Stalker quietly. "I was born here."

Everyone gaped at him. Dorimant got his breath back first.

"You mean you're actually a DeFerrier? I thought they were all dead!"

"They are," said Stalker. "I'm the last, now. And I prefer to use the name I made for myself. I ran away from home when I was fourteen. My family had become . . . corrupt, and I couldn't stand it any longer. But this house is still my home, and I want it."

Hawk thought furiously. He and Fisher had only lived in Haven a few years, but he'd heard of the DeFerriers.

Everybody had. They were an arrogant and evil family, sexually perverse and heavily involved with black magics of the foulest kind. It took a long time to prove anything against them; they were after all an old, established family, with friends in high places. But then children began to disappear. The Guard finally forced their way into the DeFerrier house, and what they found there shocked even the hardest Guards. . . . Three DeFerriers were hanged for murder, and two more were torn to pieces in the streets while trying to escape. The others had all died in prison, one way or another. And this was the family that had produced the legendary Adam Stalker, hero and avenger of evil. . . .

"Is that all?" asked Stalker. "I really don't have anything else I wish to say."

"Yes," said Hawk, snapping alert again. "I think I'm finished now. I don't have any more questions."

"You may not have," said Lord Hightower, "but I do." He looked about him. "There are two people here who haven't been questioned under the truthspell. Don't any of you find it suspicious that these murders only began after Hawk and Fisher entered this house?"

"Oh, come on," said Fisher.

"Wait just a minute," said Dorimant. "We all know William had enemies. What better way to get to him than by the very Guards who were supposed to be defending him? Who'd ever suspect them?"

"That's ridiculous!" said Hawk.

"Is it?" said Visage. "We've all had to answer under the truthspell. Why shouldn't you?"

"Very well," said Fisher. "I didn't kill Blackstone and Bowman. Hawk, did you kill them?"

"No," said Hawk. "I didn't."

There was a long silence.

"Well, that was a waste of a good truthspell," said Stalker.

"Right," said Dorimant. "We're no nearer finding the murderer than when we started."

"It wasn't a complete waste," said Hawk. "At least now we know how Blackstone died."

"And we know the murderer isn't one of us," said Visage.

"There's no one else in this house," said Gaunt. "There can't be. One of us has to be the killer."

"You heard the answers," said Hawk. "Everyone here denied being the murderer."

Gaunt frowned unhappily. "Maybe you didn't word the questions correctly."

"Grabbing at straws," growled Lord Hightower.

"If the murderer isn't one of us, then he must be hiding somewhere in the house," said Dorimant. "It's the only explanation!"

"There's no one else here!" snapped Fisher. "Hawk and I have been through every room, and there isn't a hiding place we haven't checked. There's no one here but us."

"Exactly," said Gaunt. "My wards are up and secure. No one could have got in without my knowing about it, and they certainly couldn't have moved about the house without setting off a dozen security spells. There can't be anyone else here!"

"All right then, maybe the truthspell was defective!" said Hawk. "That's the only other answer I can see!"

"I am not in the habit of casting defective spells," said Gaunt coldly. "My truthspell was effective, while it lasted."

Fisher looked at him quickly. "While it lasted? You mean it's over? I thought we had twenty-five minutes."

Gaunt shrugged. "The more people involved, the greater the strain on the spell. It's over now."

"Can you cast another?" asked Dorimant.

"Certainly," said Gaunt. "But not for another twenty-four hours."

"Great," said Hawk. "Just great."

"All right," said Stalker. "What do we do now?"

"There is one place we didn't check as thoroughly as the others," said Fisher suddenly. "The kitchen."

Hawk shrugged. "You saw for yourself; there wasn't anywhere to hide."

"I think we ought to check it anyway. Just to be sure."

Hawk looked at Gaunt, who shrugged. Hawk sighed and got to his feet. "All right, Fisher, let's take another look." She nodded, and got to her feet. Hawk glared round at the guests. "Everyone else, stay here; that's an order. I don't want anyone leaving this room till we get back. Come on, Fisher."

They left the parlour and went out into the hall, closing the door behind them. Gaunt and his guests sat in silence, lost in their own thoughts. After a while, Visage stirred uncomfortably in her chair, then rose suddenly to her feet.

"I really think we should stay here," said Gaunt. "It would be safer."

"I have to go to the bathroom," said Visage quietly, her cheeks crimson. "And no, I can't wait."

"I don't think you should go off on your own," said Dorimant.

"Quite right," said Lord Hightower. He turned to his wife. "Why don't you and I go up with her? Just to keep her company, so to speak?"

"Of course," said Lady Elaine. "You don't mind, do you, dear?"

Visage smiled, and shook her head. "I think I'd feel a lot safer, knowing I wasn't on my own."

"Don't be too long," said Gaunt. "We don't want to upset Captain Hawk, do we?"

Lord Hightower snorted loudly, but said nothing. He and his wife got to their feet and followed Visage out of the parlour. Dorimant stirred uncertainly in his chair. He would have liked to go with her too, to be sure she was safe, but the poor girl wouldn't want a crowd following her to the toilet. Besides, the Hightowers would look after her. Dorimant sank back in his chair and tried to think about something else. He felt a little better, now that Hawk and Fisher knew about the evidence he'd been concealing. Even if it didn't seem to have helped much. He glanced surreptitiously at Katherine. How could she have done it? To kneel beside her dead husband, and drive his own dagger into his chest . . . Dorimant shuddered.

"The wineglass worries me," he said finally. "If the wine wasn't poisoned . . ."

"It wasn't," said Gaunt flatly. "I tasted some myself."

"The wine . . ." said Katherine suddenly. Everyone looked at her. Katherine looked into the empty fireplace, frowning. "William didn't drink much, even at private parties. It was a rule of his. He'd already told me he'd had enough for one evening . . . but he had a fresh glass of wine in his hand when he went upstairs to change. So who gave him that glass . . . ?"

"I don't remember," said Dorimant. "I wasn't really watching." He looked at the others, and they all shook their heads.

"I'm sure I saw who it was," said Katherine, frowning. "But I can't remember. . . . I can't . . ."

"Take it easy," said Stalker. "It'll come to you, if you don't try and force it."

"It's probably not that important anyway," said Dorimant.

Hawk and Fisher checked the kitchen thoroughly from top to bottom, and found nothing and no one. There were no hidden passages, no hiding places, and nothing that looked even remotely suspicious. Not that they'd expected to find anything. Hawk and Fisher had just needed an excuse to go off on their own so that they could talk in private. They leaned back against the sink and looked gloomily about them.

"Hightower was right," said Fisher. "Much as I hate to admit it. The truthspell didn't get us anywhere. The new angle on Blackstone's death is all very interesting, but we're still no nearer finding his killer."

"Maybe," said Hawk, "and maybe not. I wouldn't know a clue if I fell over it, but I know a guilty face when I see one. Hightower's hiding something. He was jumpy as hell when he first discovered we were all stuck here for the night, and he was almost in a panic at the thought of a truthspell. There was something he didn't want to talk about. . . ."

"You didn't ask him many questions," said Fisher.

"He wouldn't have answered them if I had."

"We could have leaned on him."

Hawk smiled. "Do you honestly think we could make Lord Roderik Hightower say one damned thing he didn't want to?"

Fisher smiled reluctantly. "I see your point. Besides, there's no actual evidence that whatever's worrying him has anything to do with the murders. Old soldiers and politicians always have something to hide. After all, you asked him if he killed Blackstone and Bowman, and he said *no*. Didn't even hesitate."

Hawk scowled, thinking. "How do we know Gaunt actually cast a truthspell? Maybe . . . No. No, it worked all right; I tested it myself."

"Maybe he only cast it on you," said Fisher.

"Maybe. And maybe we're both getting paranoid."

"There is that."

"Let's get back to the parlour," said Hawk. "I don't like leaving them alone too long. I'll hit them with some more questions; try and break someone's story. Hightower's hiding something. I'd stake my career on it."

"We are," said Fisher dryly. "We are."

Visage waited alone on the landing, not far from the bathroom door. The Lady Elaine was taking her turn in the bathroom, while Lord Roderik had gone back to his room to change into more suitable clothes. The landing was still lit by only the one lamp, and the shadows seemed very dark. Visage glanced nervously about her. She wished the Lord and Lady would hurry up.

She shivered suddenly, and wrapped her arms around her. The house was still full of the sweltering summer heat, but Visage kept finding cold spots. She bit her lip and frowned unhappily. She didn't like Gaunt's house. She hadn't liked it from the moment she first crossed the threshold, but now she knew why. The DeFerriers might be dead and gone, but their house still held dark memories locked into its stone and timber. It was hard to think of a man like Stalker being a DeFerrier, but she didn't doubt it for a minute. Despite all the songs and legends, and even though he was always studiously polite to her, she'd never warmed to him. Visage had never known what William saw in him. She'd never liked Stalker. He had cold eyes.

She looked along the landing to what had been William's door. Poor William. He'd had such hopes, such dreams. . . . And poor Edward had died right there on the landing, at the top of the stairs. She looked at the ragged bloodstains on the carpet, and then looked away. She felt sorry for Edward, now he was gone. She shouldn't have said those awful things about him. They were all true, but she shouldn't have said them.

She heard footsteps behind her and turned, smiling, expecting to see Lord Roderik. Her smile faltered.

"I'm sorry," said the low, growling voice, "but you could tell them what I am. I can't allow that. I'm so sorry, Visage."

Visage started to back away, and stammered out the first few words of a defensive spell, but there wasn't enough time. Something awful surged out of the shadows towards her, and blood flew on the still, hot air.

Hawk and Fisher pounded up the stairs to the landing, cold steel in their hands. The screams they'd heard had already stopped, and Hawk had a sick feeling that he was going to be too late again.

Not another one. Please, not another one.

He stopped suddenly at the top of the steps, and Fisher bumped into him from behind. The witch Visage lay face down in the middle of the landing. Hawk moved cautiously forward, Fisher at his side. They looked quickly about them, but there was no sign of the attacker. Hawk knelt down beside Visage while Fisher stood guard. There was blood all around the witch's body. Hawk took a handful of her hair and gently lifted her head. Visage's eyes were wide and staring. Her throat had been torn out. Hawk lowered her face back onto the bloody carpet.

"And that's three," he said tiredly. "We've lost another one."

"You should be getting used to that by now," said Lord Hightower.

Hawk and Fisher straightened up quickly to find Hightower watching them from the door to his room. Hawk opened his mouth to say something, and then stopped as he heard a faint creaking sound behind him. He and Fisher spun round, weapons at the ready, to find Lady Elaine watching from the bathroom door. Her face was pale and shocked. She moved slowly forward to stand with her husband, her eyes never leaving Visage's body.

"What the hell were you all doing up here?" yelled Hawk, lowering his axe. "I told you to stay in the bloody parlour!"

"The witch had to go to the bathroom," said Hightower stiffly. "We came with her to protect her."

"Didn't do a very good job," said Fisher. "Did you?"

"Where were you when Visage died?" said Hawk.

"I was in the bathroom," said Lady Elaine.

"I was in my room, changing," said Lord Roderik.

Hawk stared at them incredulously. "You left her out here on her own?"

"It was only for a moment," said Hightower.

There were footsteps behind them, and then Dorimant came forward to kneel beside Visage's body. He reached out a hand to touch her face, and his fingers came back flecked with blood.

"She was so frightened," he said softly. "I told her there was nothing to worry about. I told her I'd look after her, and she trusted me."

Hawk looked past Dorimant. Gaunt and Stalker were standing together at the top of the stairs. Hawk glared about him.

"Where the hell were you all? What took you so long to get here?"

Nobody said anything. They looked away rather than meet his gaze, but Hawk had already seen the answer in their faces. No one had wanted to be first on the scene, for fear of being accused.

You and your partner have a reputation for violence. . . .

"Did any of you see anything?" asked Hawk. "Did anyone hear anything?"

"Only her screams," said Stalker. "I knew we shouldn't have let her go, but we all thought she'd be safe with the Hightowers."

"You left her alone," said Dorimant. He raised his head slowly and looked at Lord Hightower. "She was afraid, and you went off and left her alone in the dark. You bastard."

He threw himself at Hightower, and they fell heavily to the floor. Dorimant flailed away wildly with his fists, and then got his hands round Hightower's throat. Lord Roderik choked and gagged, tearing at Dorimant's hands. Hawk started forward, and then Hightower braced himself and flung Dorimant away. He flew backwards, and slammed up against the opposite wall. Hawk and Fisher got to him before he could go after Hightower again.

"That's enough!" said Hawk sharply. "I know how you feel, but that's enough."

Dorimant started to cry. His whole body shook from the force of the racking sobs. Fisher patted him on the shoulder, but he didn't even feel it. Hawk shook his head slowly.

What a mess . . .

Hightower got to his feet, with his wife's help, and fingered his throat gingerly. "Well?" he said loudly. "Aren't you going to arrest him? He assaulted me. I have witnesses."

"Shut your face," said Hawk. "He only beat me to it by a couple of seconds." He turned his back on Hightower, and then looked about him. "Wait a minute; where's Katherine?"

Everyone looked around, but she was nowhere to be seen.

Gaunt frowned. "She was with us in the parlour when we heard the screams. I thought she was right behind us."

Hawk's breath caught in his throat. He turned and ran back down the stairs, Fisher close behind him. He charged down the hall, kicked open the parlour door, and then skidded to a halt just inside the door. Katherine Blackstone was sitting in her chair by the empty fireplace, just as he'd last seen her. Only now there was a knife sunk deep into her chest, the hilt protruding between her breasts. The front of her dress was soaked with blood. Her head was sunk forward, and her staring eyes saw nothing, nothing at all.

6

Killer's Rage

Hawk glared furiously about him, but there was no trace of any attacker. Fisher moved forward and bent over Katherine. She checked briefly for a pulse, and then looked back at Hawk and shook her head. Hawk cursed softly. There was a clatter of feet outside in the hall, and Hawk turned quickly to face the door.

"That's close enough!" he said tightly. "Stand where you are."

Gaunt and his guests stumbled to a halt as they took in the gleaming steel axe held at the ready in Hawk's hand.

"What is it?" said Gaunt. "What's happened?"

"Katherine Blackstone is dead," said Hawk. "Murdered. I want all of you to come into the parlour slowly and in single file, keeping your hands where I can see them."

"Who the hell do you think you're talking to . . ." began the Lady Elaine.

"Shut up and move," said Hawk.

Lady Elaine took in his cold, determined face and did as she was told. The others followed her into the parlour, giving Hawk and his axe as wide a berth as possible. Hawk backed slowly away as they filed into the parlour. There was a horrified murmur as they saw Katherine's body.

"She can't have been killed," said Hightower faintly. "It's just not possible."

"Is that right?" said Fisher. "I suppose she committed suicide too?"

"But how could the killer have got down from the landing without anyone seeing him?" said Gaunt. "No one passed us on the stairs, and there's no other way down. Katherine was perfectly all right when we went running out of the parlour to investigate Visage's screams."

"Nevertheless," said Hawk, "she's still dead."

"Maybe she did commit suicide," said Stalker suddenly. "Her husband and her lover had both been killed. . . ."

"No," said Dorimant flatly. "Katherine wasn't like that. She was a fighter; always had been. Once she got over the shock of Edward's death, all she could think of was revenge. She'd already started working on how William could have been killed. . . ." He broke off, and looked a little confused. He put a hand to his forehead and swayed slightly on his feet. "Do you think I could sit down, Captain Hawk? I feel a little . . . upset."

"All right," said Hawk. "Everybody find a chair and sit down, but keep your hands in plain sight. Sir Stalker, lay your sword down on the floor by your feet, and don't touch it again until I tell you to."

Stalker studied him carefully a moment, and then nodded and followed Hawk's instructions. Fisher watched unblinkingly until Stalker was sitting in his chair with his sword at his feet, and only then lowered her sword. Stalker didn't even look in her direction. Soon everyone except

Hawk and Fisher had found themselves a chair. The two Guards stood on either side of Katherine Blackstone.

"All right," said Hawk. "Let me see if I've got this straight. Lord and Lady Hightower were up on the landing with Visage. Stalker, Gaunt, Dorimant, and Katherine were all down here in the parlour. The Lady Elaine went into the bathroom, Lord Hightower went into his bedroom, and Visage was left alone on the landing. Shortly afterwards, she was attacked and killed. Fisher and I heard her screams just as we were leaving the kitchen. We ran up the stairs to find Visage already dead, and her attacker gone. Lord and Lady Hightower came out onto the landing to see what had happened, and those in the parlour came running out into the hall. While they were leaving the parlour, or shortly afterward, Katherine was stabbed to death."

"We must have missed something," said Fisher. "Put like that, the two murders couldn't have happened. It just wasn't possible."

"It has to be possible!" Hawk hefted his axe angrily. "I don't believe this. Four people have been murdered, in a house full of witnesses, and nobody sees anything!"

He glared round at Gaunt and his guests, and then turned disgustedly away to look at Katherine. He frowned slightly. He'd thought at first that she might have been stabbed somewhere else and then brought back and dumped in her chair, but while the front of her dress was soaked with blood, there were no bloodstains to be seen anywhere else. So, the killer must have struck no more than a few seconds after the others had left the parlour. . . . Hawk scowled. It was possible. Everyone had been so intent on what was happening on the landing that they wouldn't have noticed someone sneaking into the parlour. But how the hell had the killer got down from the landing to the hall? Hawk shook his head and leaned over Katherine to get a closer look at the dagger that had killed her. The hilt jutted obscenely from between her breasts. Hawk noted that the blow had been struck with professional skill; just under the sternum and straight into the heart. The hilt itself was a standard metal grip wrapped in leather, with nothing to distinguish it from a thousand others just like it. Hawk straightened up and turned reluctantly back to the sorcerer and his guests.

"Some of you must have seen something, even if you don't recognise it. Have any of you seen or heard anything out of the ordinary, no matter how silly or trivial it may sound?"

There was a long silence as they all looked at each other, and then Stalker stirred thoughtfully.

"It could be nothing," he said slowly, "but up on the landing I could have sworn I smelt something."

"You smelt something?" said Hawk. "What did it smell like?"

"I don't know. It was a musky, animal smell."

Fisher nodded slowly. "Visage said she smelt something earlier on, just after Bowman's death. She wasn't sure what it was."

"I'm not sure either," said Stalker. "But it was definitely some kind of animal. . . ."

"Like a wolf?" said Hawk suddenly.

Stalker looked at him, and nodded grimly. "Yes . . . like a wolf."

"This is ridiculous," said Gaunt. "There are no wolves in Haven. And anyway, how could a wolf have got into my house, past all my wards and defences?"

"Quite simply," said Hawk. "You invited him in."

"Oh, my God," said Lady Elaine. "A werewolf . . ."

"Yes," said Hawk. "A shapeshifter. It all makes sense

now, if you think about it. What kind of murderer kills sometimes with a knife and sometimes like a wild animal? A man who is sometimes a wolf. A werewolf.''

"And there's a full moon tonight," said Fisher.

"You've had some experience in tracking down werewolves, haven't you?" said Dorimant.

"Experience," said Hightower bitterly. "Oh, yes, Hawk knows all about werewolves, don't you, Captain? How many this time, Captain? How many more of us are going to die because of your incompetence?" His wife put a gentle hand on his arm, and he subsided reluctantly, still glaring at Hawk.

"I don't understand," said Gaunt. "Are you seriously suggesting that one of us is a werewolf?"

"Yes," said Hawk flatly. "It's the only answer that fits."

They all looked at each other, as though expecting to see telltale fur and fangs and claws.

Dorimant looked at Gaunt. "Can't your magic tell you which one of us is the werewolf?"

Gaunt stirred uncomfortably. "Not really. There are such spells, but they're rather out of my field."

"There are other means of detecting a werewolf," said Hawk.

"Oh, of course," said Gaunt quickly. "Wolfsbane, for example. A lycanthrope should react very strongly to wolfsbane."

"I was thinking more of silver," said Hawk. "Do you have any silver weapons in the house, sir sorcerer?"

"There's a silver dagger somewhere in my laboratory," said Gaunt. "At least, there used to be. I haven't used it in a long time."

"All right," said Hawk patiently. "Go and look for it.

No, wait a minute. I don't want anyone going off on their own. Fisher and I will come with you.''

"No," said Lord Hightower flatly. "I don't trust you, Hawk. You were involved with a werewolf before. How do we know you didn't get bitten and become infected with the werewolf curse?"

"That's crazy!" said Fisher angrily. "Hawk's no werewolf!"

"Take it easy," said Hawk quickly. "Lord Hightower is right. Until we can prove otherwise, no one is above suspicion. Absolutely no one."

Hightower stiffened slightly. "Are you suggesting . . ."

"Why not?" said Hawk. "Anyone can become a werewolf."

"How dare you," said Hightower softly, furiously. "You of all people should remember what good cause I have to hate shapeshifters."

For a moment, nobody said anything.

"Why don't you come with me, Rod," said Gaunt quietly. "I'm sure I'll feel a lot safer with an old soldier like you along to watch my back."

"Of course," said Hightower gruffly. "You come along too, Elaine. You'll be safer with us."

Lady Elaine nodded, and she and her husband followed Gaunt out of the parlour and into the hall. The door closed quietly behind them.

"A werewolf," said Dorimant slowly. "I never really believed in such creatures."

"I wasn't sure I believed in vampires," said Fisher. "Until I met one."

"Werewolves are magical creatures," said Stalker. "And there's only one of us left with magical abilities. Interesting, that, isn't it?"

Hawk looked at him. "Are you suggesting that Gaunt . . . ?"

"Why not?" said Stalker. "I never did trust sorcerers. You heard how those people died in the Hook, didn't you?"

Hawk and Fisher looked at each other thoughtfully. Fisher raised an eyebrow, and Hawk shrugged slightly. He knew she was thinking of the succubus. Hawk tried to consider the point dispassionately. He'd assumed the succubus had been responsible for the deaths in the Hook, but they could just as easily have been the result of a werewolf on a killing spree. And Gaunt was an alchemist; he'd know about poisons. They only had his word that Blackstone's wine hadn't been poisoned. In fact, if the sorcerer was a werewolf he could probably have tasted poisoned wine and not taken any harm from it. And perhaps most important of all, Gaunt had been one of the last people in the parlour with Katherine. . . .

Hawk scowled. It all made a kind of sense. He glanced at the closed parlour door and wondered if he should go after them. No, better not. Not yet, anyway. Hightower could look after himself, and it wasn't as if there was any real proof against Gaunt. . . . Hawk sat back in his chair and silently cursed his indecision. He was a Guard, and he couldn't make a move without some kind of proof.

Lord and Lady Hightower waited impatiently in the library while Gaunt searched his laboratory for the silver dagger. Gaunt had politely but firmly refused to let them enter the laboratory with him. Lady Elaine understood. All men liked to have one room they could think of as their own; a private den they could retreat to when the world got a little too hard to cope with. Lady Elaine watched her husband pacing up and down, and wished she could say something to calm him. She'd never seen him so worried before. It was the werewolf, of course. Ever since Paul's death, Roderik had been obsessed with finding the creatures, and making them pay in blood. Despite his endless hunts he'd never found but one, and that one escaped, after killing three of his men. Now he finally had a chance to come face to face with a werewolf, and the odds were it was going to be one of his friends. No wonder he was torn. . . .

Elaine sighed quietly. She was starting to feel some of the pressure herself. The unending heat was getting to her, and she jumped at every sudden noise. She was tired and her muscles ached, but she couldn't relax, even for a minute. It wasn't just the deaths. They were upsetting, of course, but it was the horrid feeling of helplessness that was most disturbing. No matter what anyone said or did, no matter what theories they came up with, people kept dying. No wonder her head ached unmercifully and Roderik's temper kept shortening by the minute. Elaine sighed again, a little louder this time, and sat down in one of the chairs. She tried to look calm and relaxed, in the hope that Roderik would follow her example, but he didn't.

Elaine hoped they'd got it right this time, and that the killer really was a werewolf. Roderik needed so badly to kill a werewolf. Perhaps when he saw the creature lying dead and broken at his feet he'd be able to forget about Paul's death and start thinking about his own life again. Perhaps . . .

Roderik suddenly stopped pacing, and stood very still. His shoulders were hunched and his head was bowed, and Elaine could see a faint sheen of sweat on his face. His hands were clenched into fists.

"Why doesn't he hurry up?" muttered Roderik. "What's taking him so long?"

"It's only been a few minutes, my dear," said Elaine. "Give the man time."

"It's hot," said Roderik. He didn't look at her, and didn't even seem to have heard her. "So damned hot. And close. I can't stand it. The rooms are all too small. . . ."

"Rod?"

"I've got to get out of here. I've got to get out of this place."

Elaine rose to her feet and moved quickly over to take his arm. Roderik looked at her frowningly, as though he knew her face but couldn't quite place it. And then recognition moved slowly in his eyes, and he reached across to gently pat her hand on his arm.

"I'm sorry, my dear. It's the heat, and the waiting. I hate being cooped up in here, in this house."

"It's only until the morning, dear. Then the spell will be gone and we can leave."

"I don't think I can wait that long," said Roderik. He looked at her for a long moment, his eyes tender but strangely distant. "Elaine, my dear, whatever happens, I love you. Never doubt it."

"And I love you, Rod. But don't talk anymore. It's just the heat upsetting you."

"No," said Roderik. "It's not just the heat."

His face twisted suddenly and his eyes squeezed shut. He bent sharply forward, and wrapped his arms around himself. Elaine grabbed him by the shoulders to stop him falling.

"Rod? What is it? Do you have a pain?"

He pushed her away from him, and she staggered back a step. Hightower swayed from side to side, bent almost double. "Get out of here! Get away from me! Please!"

"Rod! What's the matter?"

"It hurts . . . it hurts, Elaine! The moonlight's in my mind! Run, Elaine, run!"

"No! I can't leave you like this, Rod. . . ."

And then he turned his shaggy head and looked at her. Elaine's eyes widened and her throat went dry. He growled, deep in his throat. The air was heavy with the smell of musk and hair. Elaine turned to run. The werewolf caught her long before she got to the door.

In the parlour, Stalker poured himself another glass of wine, and looked thoughtfully at the clock on the mantelpiece.

"They're taking their time, aren't they? How long does it take to find one dagger and some herbs in a jar?"

Hawk nodded slowly. "Not this long. We'll give them a few more minutes, but if they're not back then, I think we'd better go and take a look for ourselves."

Stalker nodded and sipped at his wine. Fisher continued to pace up and down before the closed parlour door. Hawk smiled slightly. Fisher never had cared much for waiting. Dorimant was sitting slumped in a chair, as far away from Katherine as he could get. His hands were clasped tightly together in his lap, and every now and again he would look quickly at the tablecloth covering Katherine's body, and then look away. Hawk frowned. Dorimant wasn't holding together too well, but you couldn't really blame him. The tension and the uncertainty were getting to everyone, and the night seemed to be never-ending. It was only to be expected that someone would start to crack. Hawk looked at the clock on the mantelpiece and chewed worriedly at his lower lip. Gaunt was taking too long.

"All right," he said sharply. "That's it. Let's go and find out what the hell's happening. Everyone stick together. No one is to go off on their own, no matter what."

Stalker reached for his sword before getting to his feet. Hawk started to say something, and then decided against it. If the others had been attacked, he was going to need Stalker's expertise with a sword to back him up. Hawk headed for the door, and Fisher opened it for him. He smiled slightly as he saw she'd already drawn her sword. He drew his axe and stepped cautiously out into the hall. The library door stood slightly ajar, and the hall was empty. Hawk crossed over to the library, the others close behind him. He pushed the library door open. Lady Elaine Hightower lay in a crumpled heap on the floor. Her throat had been torn out. There was no sign of Gaunt or Roderik.

Hawk moved cautiously forward into the library, glaring about him. Fisher moved silently at his side, the lamplight shining golden on her sword blade. Stalker and Dorimant moved quickly in behind them. Hawk moved over to the laboratory door, and felt his hackles rise as he realised the door was standing slightly ajar. Gaunt would never have left that door open, for any reason. . . . A wolf's howl sounded suddenly from inside the laboratory, followed by the sound of breaking glass and rending wood. Hawk ran forward, kicked the door open, and burst into the laboratory.

The werewolf threw himself at the succubus's throat, and they fell sprawling to the floor, snarling and clawing. They slammed up against a wooden bench and overturned it. Alchemical equipment fell to the floor and shattered. Hawk looked quickly at the pentacle on the far side of the room. Its blue chalk lines were smudged and broken. Gaunt lay unmoving on the floor, not far away. Hawk hurried over to crouch beside him, keeping a careful eye on the werewolf and the succubus as they raged back and forth across the laboratory. Fisher and Stalker stood to-

gether in the doorway, swords in hand, guarding the only
exit. Dorimant watched wide-eyed from behind them.

The succubus tore at the werewolf with her clawed
hands. Long rents appeared in the werewolf's sides, only
to close again in a matter of seconds. The succubus's eyes
blazed with a sudden golden light and flames roared up
around the werewolf. But the sorcerous fire couldn't con-
sume him. He threw himself at her again, and his fangs
and claws left bloody furrows on her perfect skin. The
succubus's head snapped forward, and she sank her teeth
into the werewolf's throat. He howled with rage and pain,
and flung her away. They quickly regained their balance
and circled each other warily.

Fisher lifted her sword and started forward from the
doorway, but Hawk waved her back. Cold steel was no
defence against a werewolf, let alone an enraged succubus. Gaunt stirred slowly beside him, and Hawk took the
sorcerer by the shoulder and turned him over. He had a
few nasty cuts and bruises but otherwise looked unharmed. Hawk shook him roughly, and the sorcerer
groaned and tried to sit up.

The succubus screamed, and Hawk turned just in time
to see the werewolf rip out her throat with one savage twist
of his jaws. Horribly, the succubus didn't die. She stood
where she was, backed up against the laboratory wall, and
blood ran down her chest in a steady stream. The werewolf
hit her again, and blood flew on the air, but still she didn't
die. And then Gaunt said a single Word of Power, and she
slumped forward and fell lifeless to the floor. The werewolf sniffed warily at the unmoving body, and then turned
to snarl at Fisher and Stalker, still blocking the only door.

"I had to do it," said Gaunt. "She was bound to me.
She couldn't die until I let her go. I couldn't bear to lose

her, but I couldn't let her suffer. . . ." Tears ran down his face, but he didn't seem to notice them.

Hawk grabbed him by the arm and dragged him to his feet. "The silver dagger," he hissed. "Did you find the silver dagger?"

Gaunt shook his head dazedly. "No . . . not yet."

"You have to find it!" said Hawk. "We'll try and keep the beast occupied."

"Yes," said Gaunt. "The dagger. I'll kill the creature." His eyes suddenly focused, and he was back in control of himself again. He looked hard at the werewolf, crouched beside the dead succubus. "Who is that? Who wore the mark of the beast?"

"Hightower," said Hawk. "Lord Roderik Hightower. I recognise what's left of his clothes."

Gaunt nodded slowly and moved away to start searching through the drawers of a nearby table. The werewolf turned his shaggy head to watch Gaunt, but made no move to attack him. The werewolf's fur was matted with drying blood, and his claws and teeth had a crimson sheen.

"How?" said Dorimant shakily. "How can Roderik be the werewolf? He hates the creatures; one of them killed his son. . . ."

"Exactly," said Hawk. "He hated them so much he spent all his time leading expeditions to track them down and kill them. In the end, it became an obsession with him. That's why the army made him resign. As I understand it, he only found one werewolf, but it seems one was enough. The creature must have bitten him."

"And whoever feels a werewolf's bite, shall become a wolf when the moon is bright," said Fisher. "The poor bastard."

"Ironic," said Stalker. He hefted his sword, and the werewolf snarled soundlessly at him.

"But why did Roderik want to kill all those people?" said Dorimant. "They were his friends."

"Werewolves kill because they have to," said Hawk. "When the moon is full, the killing rage fills their mind until there's nothing left but wolf. God knows how Hightower managed to hide it this long. Maybe he just went off and locked himself up somewhere safe until the full moon was past and his madness was over."

"And then we trapped him here," said Fisher. "With a fresh supply of victims, and no way out . . ."

"It's not your fault," said Stalker. "You couldn't have known. In the meantime, it's up to us to stop him, before he kills again."

"Stop him?" said Hawk. "There's only one thing that will stop a werewolf, and Gaunt isn't even sure he's got one. The best we can hope to do is slow the beast down."

"Let me talk to him," said Stalker. "I've known Roderik on and off for more than twenty years. Maybe he'll listen to me."

He lowered his sword and stepped forward. The werewolf crouched before him, watching him unblinkingly. The beast stood on two legs like a man, wrapped in the tatters of a man's clothing, but his stance wasn't in any way human. His body was long and wiry and covered with thick bristly hair. The hands were elongated paws, with long curved claws. The narrow tapering muzzle was full of teeth, and blood dripped from the grinning jaws. The werewolf's eyes were a startling blue, but there was nothing human in their unwavering gaze. He growled once, hungrily, and Stalker stopped where he was.

"Why didn't you come to me?" said Stalker quietly. "I would have helped you, Rod. I'd have found someone who could take the curse away from you."

The werewolf rose slowly out of his crouch and padded forward. His hands flexed eagerly.

"He can't hear you," said Hawk. "There's nothing left now but the beast."

The werewolf sprang forward, and Stalker met him with his sword. The long steel blade cut into the werewolf's chest and out again, and didn't even slow him down. He knocked Stalker to the ground and dashed the sword from his hand. Stalker grabbed the werewolf by the throat with both hands, and fought to keep the grinning jaws away from his throat. The werewolf's quick panting breath slapped against his face, thick with the stench of fresh blood and rotting meat. Fisher stepped forward and thrust her sword through the werewolf's ribs. The beast howled with pain and fury. Fisher pulled back her sword for another thrust, and then cursed as the wound healed itself in seconds. Hawk moved in and swung his axe double-handed. The heavy blade sank deep into the werewolf's shoulder, smashing the collarbone. The werewolf tried to pull away, but Stalker held on grimly, digging his fingers into the beast's throat. Fisher cut at the werewolf again and again. The beast sank his claws into Stalker's chest. Hawk pulled out his axe for another blow, and the werewolf broke Stalker's hold and jumped back out of range. A jagged wound showed clearly in the beast's shoulder, but it didn't bleed. There was a series of faint popping sounds as the broken bones reknit themselves, and then the wound closed and was gone.

We're not going to stop him, thought Hawk slowly. *There's not a damn thing we can do to stop him. . . .*

The werewolf lowered his shaggy head and sprang forward. Hawk and Fisher braced themselves, weapons at the ready. Stalker looked to where he'd dropped his sword, but it was too far away. The werewolf went for his throat.

Stalker ducked under the werewolf's leap and gutted the beast with a dagger he snatched from his boot at the last moment. The werewolf crashed heavily to the floor, screaming in an almost human voice. He lay helpless for a moment as the wound healed, and Stalker dropped his dagger, leant over the beast, and taking a firm hold at neck and tail, lifted the werewolf over his head. The beast kicked and struggled but couldn't break free. Stalker held it there, his muscles creaking and groaning under the strain. Sweat ran down his face with the effort, but he wouldn't let the beast go. As long as the werewolf couldn't reach anyone, he was harmless. Pain ran jaggedly through Stalker's arms and chest from the weight of the beast, but he wouldn't give in. He wouldn't give in. Hawk and Fisher watched in awe. This was the Stalker they'd heard about, the legendary hero who'd never known defeat.

And then Gaunt stepped forward, a silver dagger gleaming in his hand. Stalker slammed the werewolf to the floor with the last of his strength. The impact stunned the werewolf for a moment, and Gaunt plunged the silver dagger into the beast's chest, just under the breastbone. Gaunt and Stalker stepped quickly back as the werewolf writhed and twisted on the laboratory floor. He scrabbled forward a few feet, and then suddenly coughed blood. It was a quiet, almost apologetic sound. The werewolf lay still and closed his eyes. The wolf shape stirred and shifted. The fur and fangs and claws slowly disappeared, and bones creaked softly as their shape changed. When it was over, Lord Roderik Hightower lay still on the floor, curled around the silver dagger embedded in his heart. Gaunt knelt down beside him.

"Why didn't you tell us, Rod?" he said quietly. "We were your friends; we'd have found some way to help you."

Hightower opened his eyes and looked at the sorcerer. He smiled slightly, and there was blood on his lips. "I liked being a wolf. I felt young again. Is Elaine dead?"

"Yes," said Gaunt. "You killed her."

"My poor Elaine. I never could tell her. . . ."

"You should have told us, Rod."

Hightower raised an eyebrow tiredly. "You should have told us about your succubus, but you didn't. We all have our secrets, Gaunt. Some of them are just easier to live with than others."

Gaunt nodded slowly. "Why did you kill William, Rod?"

Hightower laughed soundlessly. "I didn't," he said quietly. And then he died.

Gaunt slowly straightened up and looked at the others. "I don't understand," he said slowly. "Why should he lie about it? He knew he was dying."

"He didn't lie," said Hawk. Everyone looked at him sharply, and he smiled grimly. "All along I've been saying this case didn't make sense, and I was right. The evidence didn't tie together because there wasn't just one murderer. There were two."

7

A Hidden Evil

The parlour seemed somehow larger, now there were so few people left to sit in it. The chair with Katherine's body had been pushed to the rear of the room. The still, sheeted figure sat slumped in its chair like a sleeping ghost. The two Guards and their suspects sat in a rough semicircle around the empty fireplace. They sat in silence, looking at each other with tired, suspicious eyes. Hawk and Fisher sat side by side. Hawk was scowling thoughtfully, while Fisher glared at everyone impartially, her sword resting across her knees. Dorimant sat on the edge of his chair, mopping at his face with a handkerchief. The heat was worse if anything, and the parlour was almost unbearably close and stuffy. Gaunt sat stiffly in his chair, staring at nothing. He hadn't said a word since they left the laboratory. Stalker handed him a glass of wine, and the sorcerer looked at it dully. Stalker had to coax him into taking the first sip, but after that Gaunt carried on drinking mechanically, until the glass was empty. Stalker noted Hawk's disapproving frown and leant forward conspiratorially.

"Don't worry," he said quietly. "The wine contains a

strong sedative. Let him sleep off the shock; it's the best thing for him.''

Hawk nodded slowly. "You must be very skilled at sleight of hand, sir Stalker; I didn't see you drop anything into his wine.''

Stalker grinned. "I didn't. It's a variation on my transformation trick with the alcohol, only this time I used the spell to change some of the wine into a sedative. Simple, but effective.''

Hawk nodded thoughtfully, and Stalker sank back in his chair. He glanced at the clock on the mantelpiece, and then looked sharply at Hawk.

"Your time's nearly up, Captain. In just under half an hour it will be dawn, and the isolation spell will collapse. If Hightower was telling the truth, you don't have much time left to find your second killer.''

"I don't need any more time," said Hawk calmly. "I know who the second murderer is.''

Everyone looked at him sharply, including Fisher. "Are you sure, Hawk?" she said carefully. "We can't afford to be wrong.''

"I'm sure," said Hawk. "Everything's finally fallen into place. I'd pretty much worked out the who and why a while back, but I still couldn't work out how it had been done . . . and without that, I couldn't make an accusation.''

"But now you've got it?" said Fisher.

"Yeah," said Hawk. He looked unhurriedly around him, letting the tension build. Stalker was watching him interestedly, his hand resting on the sword at his side. Dorimant was perched right on the edge of his chair, leaning eagerly forward. Gaunt watched quietly, sitting slumped in his chair, his eyes already drooping from the sedative Stalker had given him. Fisher was glaring at him impatiently, and Hawk decided he'd better make a start.

"Let me recap a little to begin with," said Hawk slowly. "This has been a complicated case, made even more so because right from the word *go* there were two killers, working separately, with completely unconnected motives. That's why the truthspell didn't work. I asked everyone if they killed Blackstone *and* Bowman. And of course each killer could truthfully say no; they'd only killed one man, not both.

"The first killer was of course Lord Roderik Hightower. Under the influence of the full moon, his killer's rage drove him to become a wolf and kill Edward Bowman. The choice of victim was pure chance. If Hightower hadn't found Bowman on the landing, he would undoubtedly have found someone else to attack. He killed his second victim, the witch Visage, while his wife was out of sight in the bathroom and Visage was left alone on the landing. I think he probably killed her deliberately. She'd smelt something strange on the landing after Bowman's murder, and given time she might have been able to identify what it was. So Hightower killed her, while he had the chance. By the time he killed his wife, the Lady Elaine, the werewolf in him was too strong to be denied. The killing rage must have been overpowering. It's a wonder he was able to fight it off and stay human as long as he did.

"But while all this was going on, another killer was moving among us, the man who killed William Blackstone and his wife, Katherine. Again, the case was made more complicated by outside factors. To begin with, we were distracted by the door having been apparently locked from the inside. Once Katherine admitted her part in that deception, and in the stabbing of the dead body to mislead us as to the cause of death, the situation grew a little clearer. The wineglass in Blackstone's room intrigued me. The wine had to have been poisoned, but Gaunt swore that it was harmless. He even tasted some of it himself, to prove it. But then someone secretly removed the wineglass from Blackstone's room, proving that the wine had in some way contributed to Blackstone's death. If it hadn't, why go to all the trouble and risk of removing it?''

"So William definitely was poisoned?'' said Dorimant.

"In a way,'' said Hawk. "The poison killed him, but he really died by magic.''

"That's impossible!'' snapped Gaunt. He struggled to sit up straighter, and glared at Hawk. "William was still wearing the amulet Visage made for him. It was a good amulet; I tested it myself. As long as he was wearing it, magic wouldn't work in his vicinity.''

"Exactly,'' said Hawk. "And that's why he died.''

Gaunt looked at him confusedly, and some of the fire went out of his eyes as the sedative took hold of him again. Hawk looked quickly around at the other listeners. Dorimant was leaning so far forward it was a wonder he hadn't fallen off his chair. Stalker was frowning thoughtfully. And Fisher was looking as though she'd brain him if he didn't get on with his story.

"It was a very clever scheme,'' said Hawk. "Since there was no trace of poison, if it hadn't been for Katherine's interference, we'd probably have put Blackstone's death down to natural causes. So, how did he die? It all comes down to the amulet and the glass of wine. The killer took a glass of poison and worked a transformation spell on it, so that it became a glass of perfectly normal wine. He then gave the glass to Blackstone. However, once Blackstone raised the glass to his lips, the amulet cancelled out the transformation magic, and the wine reverted to its original and deadly state. Blackstone must have died shortly after entering his bedroom. He fell to the floor, dropping the wineglass. It rolled away from the body, passed beyond the amulet's influence, and the poison became wine again. Which is why Gaunt was able to taste it quite safely. Later on, the killer went back to the room and removed the wineglass. He knew a thorough examination would reveal the wine's true nature. If everything had gone according to plan, and Blackstone's death had been accepted as a heart attack, he would probably have switched the original glass for another, containing normal wine, but as things were he was no doubt pressed for time.''

"Ingenious," said Gaunt, blinking owlishly.

"Yes, but is it practical?" said Dorimant. "Would it have worked?"

"Oh, yes," said Gaunt. "It would have worked. And that's why Katherine had to die! Just before Visage's death, Katherine was trying to remember who had given William that last glass of wine. She was sure she'd seen who it was, but she couldn't quite remember. She had to die, because the killer was afraid she might identify him."

"Right," said Hawk. "So, we've established how William Blackstone died. Now we come to the suspects. Gaunt, Dorimant, Stalker. Three suspects; but only one of you had the means and the opportunity and the motive.

"Gaunt could have worked the transformation spell on the wine. He knew about the amulet, and he is both a sorcerer and an alchemist. But he also had a succubus, with all the power and abilities that granted him. If he'd wanted Blackstone dead, there were any number of ways he could have managed it, without any danger of it being traced back to him. He certainly wouldn't have committed a murder in his own house; an investigation might have discovered his succubus, and he couldn't risk that.

"Dorimant . . . I did wonder about you for a while. You were obviously very attached to the witch Visage, and jealousy can be a powerful motive. If you thought Blackstone was all that stood between you and her . . . but you know nothing about magic. You didn't even know how a truthspell worked."

Hawk turned slowly to Stalker. "It had to be you, Stalker. You worked your transformation trick on the wine once too often. Taking the alcohol out of wine was one thing. I might have overlooked that, but changing the wine to a sedative for Gaunt was a mistake. Once I'd seen that, a lot of things suddenly fell into place. I wondered why Blackstone had taken that last glass of wine, when he'd already said he wasn't going to drink any more because he had no head for wine. He took that final glass because you told him you'd worked your trick on it to take out the alcohol. Also, when Visage was killed on the landing, you were one of the last people to leave the parlour, which meant you had plenty of time to kill Katherine, while everyone else's attention was distracted.

"It was the lack of motive that threw me for a long time, until I discovered you were a DeFerrier. Blackstone's next main cause would have been a drive against child prostitution, and those who supported it. Fisher and I were working on just such a case before we were called away to go after the Chandler Lane vampire. The word was that we were called off because we were getting too close to one of the main patrons, an influential and very respectable man with a taste for abusing children. The DeFerriers had a thing about children, didn't they? We'll never know exactly how many children were tortured and killed in their black magic rituals. You were the patron, Stalker. You were the one who had us called off. And that's why you had to kill Blackstone. During his investigation, he'd discovered your obsession with child prostitutes, and he was going to turn you over to the Guard, as soon as he had some concrete evidence to use against you. And he'd have found it, eventually. Oh, you argued with him, promised him anything and everything, but Blackstone was an honest man. You couldn't buy him, and you couldn't intimidate him, so you killed him. You couldn't have let him tell the world what you really are. It would have destroyed your reputation and your legend, and that's all you've got left to live on.

"You must have put a lot of planning into Blackstone's death, Stalker. After all, you were the one who first told Visage how to make the protective amulet. Ironic, isn't it? By wearing that amulet, he was unknowingly collaborating in his own murder. If it hadn't been for Katherine, you might well have got away with it, and your dirty little secret would have been safe. Adam Stalker, I hereby place you under arrest for the murder of William and Katherine Blackstone."

For a long moment nobody said anything, and then Stalker chuckled quietly. "I said you were good, didn't I? You worked it all out, from beginning to end. If it hadn't been for that bitch Katherine . . . I forgot how tough she was. She always could think on her feet, and she was one hell of an actress. If it hadn't been for her muddying the waters, you wouldn't have suspected a thing. But it doesn't matter. I'm not going to stand trial."

Hawk threw himself sideways out of his chair as Stalker suddenly lunged forward, sword in hand. Hawk hit the floor rolling as the sword slammed into the back of the chair where he'd been sitting. He was quickly back on his feet again, axe in hand. Fisher was also on her feet, sword at the ready. Gaunt and Dorimant watched, shocked, as

Stalker drew his sword, kicked aside his chair, and backed quickly away.

"You've got good reflexes, Hawk," said Stalker. "But you still don't stand a chance against me. The only one who could have stopped me is Gaunt, and my sedative's taken care of him. In a few minutes the isolation spell will collapse, and I'll be on my way. The Guard will find nothing but a house full of bodies, and I'll be long gone. This will be just another unsolved mystery. Haven's full of them."

"You're not going anywhere," said Fisher, lifting her sword slightly.

"You think you're going to stop me, girl?"

"Why not? I've dealt with worse than you in my time."

Stalker smiled contemptuously and stepped forward, his long sword shining brightly as it cut through the air towards her. Fisher braced herself and parried the blow, grunting at the effort it cost her. The sword was heavy, and Stalker was every bit as strong as they said he was. She cut at his unprotected leg, and he parried the blow easily. Hawk moved in to join her, swinging his axe. Stalker picked up a chair with his free hand and threw it at Hawk. One of the chair legs struck him a glancing blow to the head and he fell to the floor, stunned. Fisher threw herself at Stalker, and he stepped forward to meet her. He quickly took the advantage, and Fisher was forced to retreat round the room, blocking his sword with hers as she searched and waited for an opening in his defence that never came. She was good with a blade, but he was better.

Sparks sputtered and died on the still air, and the parlour was full of the ring of steel on steel. Hawk got to his feet and shook his head to clear it. Stalker scowled briefly. He couldn't fight them both, and he knew it. He turned suddenly and cut viciously at Dorimant, who shrank back

in his chair, unharmed. Fisher threw herself forward to
block the blow, and Stalker spun round at the last moment
and kicked her solidly under the left knee. Fisher collapsed as her leg betrayed her, groaning with agony.
Stalker drew back his sword to finish her, and then Hawk
was upon him, swinging his axe double-handed, and
Stalker had to retreat.

Stalker and Hawk stood toe to toe, their blades a flashing blur in the lamplight. Sword and axe rose and fell, cut
and parry and riposte, with no quarter asked or given. The
pace was too fast for the fight to last long. Stalker tried
every dirty trick and foul move he knew, but none of them
worked against Hawk. In the end he felt himself beginning
to slow, and grew desperate. He used the same trick once
too often, and Hawk stepped inside his guard and knocked
the sword from his hand. Stalker staggered back, nursing
his numbed hand. He leaned against the wall, breathing
hard.

"I said you were good, Hawk. Ten years ago you
wouldn't have touched me . . . but that was ten years ago."
He waited a moment while his breathing slowed and stead-
ied. "It's not really my fault, you know. You can't imagine
what it was like, growing up in this house, seeing the
things my family did. . . . What chance did I have? They
were vile, all of them, and they tried to corrupt me, too.
I couldn't stop them; I was only a child. So I ran away.
And I became a hero, to help others, because there was
no one to help me when I needed it. But still I was tainted,
full of the corruption they'd taught me. I fought it; I fought
it for years. But it was too strong, and I was too weak. . . .
I even tried to buy this house, so I could burn it to the
ground and break its hold on me. But Gaunt wouldn't sell.
It wasn't my fault. None of it was my fault! I didn't choose
to be . . . what I am."

"I saw what you did to that girl in the brothel over the Nag's Head," said Hawk. "I would have killed myself before I did such a thing."

Stalker nodded slowly. "I was never that brave. Till now. I told you I wouldn't stand trial."

He drew a dagger from his boot, turned it quickly in his hand, and thrust it deep into his heart. He fell to his knees, looked triumphantly at Hawk, and then fell forward and lay still. Hawk moved cautiously forward and stirred the body with his boot. There was no response. He knelt down and tried for a pulse. There wasn't one. Adam Stalker was dead.

"It's over," said Dorimant. "It's finally over."

"Yes," said Hawk, getting tiredly to his feet. "I think it is." He looked at Fisher. "Are you all right, lass?"

"I'll live," said Fisher dryly, flexing her aching leg.

"He was one of the best," said Dorimant, staring sadly at Stalker's body. "I never liked him, but I always admired him. He was one of the greatest heroes ever to come out of the Low Kingdoms. He really did do most of the things the legends say he did."

"Yes," said Hawk. "I know. And that's why we're going to say Hightower was responsible for all the deaths. No one really blames a werewolf. Haven needs legends like Stalker more than it needs the truth."

Dorimant nodded slowly. "I suppose you're right. A man's past should be buried with the man."

There was a sudden lurch as the house seemed to drop an inch. A subtle tension on the air was suddenly gone.

"The isolation spell," said Fisher. "It's finished. Let's get the hell out of this place."

They all looked at Gaunt, sleeping peacefully in his chair.

"You go on," said Dorimant. "I'll stick around till he

wakes up. Someone's got to brief him on the story we're going to tell. Besides . . ." Dorimant looked levelly at Hawk and Fisher. "I promised Visage I'd look after her. I don't want to leave her here, in the company of strangers."

"All right," said Hawk. "We won't be long. What will you do now, Dorimant, now that Blackstone is dead . . . ?"

"I'll think of something," said Dorimant. "If nothing else, I'll be able to dine out on this story for months."

They laughed, and then Hawk and Fisher made their goodbyes and left. They walked unhurriedly down the hall to the closed front door. Hawk hesitated a moment, and then pulled the door open. A cool breeze swept in, dispelling the heat of the long night. The sun had come up, and there were rain clouds in the early morning skies, and a hint of moisture on the air. Hawk and Fisher stood together a while, quietly enjoying the cool of the breeze.

"It was partly the heat," said Fisher finally. "It brings out the worst in people."

"Yeah," said Hawk. "But only if the evil is there to be brought out. Come on, lass, let's go."

They shut the door behind them, and walked out of the grounds and down the steep hill that led back into the shadowed heart of the city. Even in the early morning light, Haven is a dark city.